HONEY

ALSO BY
Sarah Weeks

Pie

Cheese: A Combo of "Oggie Cooder"
and "Oggie Cooder, Party Animal"

Save Me a Seat (with Gita Varadarajan)

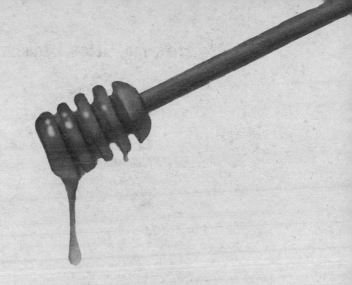

HONEY

Sarah Weeks

SCHOLASTIC INC.

For my sister, Jane
— SW

10 9 8 7 6 5 4 3 2 1   16 17 18 19 20

Printed in the U.S.A.   40
First printing 2016

The text type was set in Alisal.
Book design by Sharismar Rodriguez

Chapter One

"Knock-knock!" Teeny Nelson called through a knot hole in the high wooden fence that separated the Nelsons' yard from the Bishops'.

Melody pretended not to hear. She was on a mission. She had a serious sweet tooth and her personal candy fund was running dangerously low. That morning at breakfast her father had offered to pay her a nickel for every dandelion plant she could pull out of the lawn. Her plan was to try to earn enough money to buy herself a pack of Wild Berry Skittles — maybe even two.

"For your information, when I say 'Knock-knock,' you're supposed to say 'Who's there?'" Teeny instructed.

"For *your* information," Melody told her, "I'm busy."

"Doesn't look like you're busy," said Teeny, putting a big blue eye up to the knothole. "Looks like you're picking dandy-lions. Can I help?"

It was a Saturday morning in May. The weather in Royal, Indiana, had been unseasonably warm for weeks, and the promise of summer hung in the air. A pair of cardinals was busy building a nest in a rhododendron near the northeast corner of the Bishops' house, and somewhere down the street a lawn mower droned like a giant bumblebee.

"You'll need to use the weed fork," Melody's father had explained. "You have to get out the whole root, otherwise the dandelion will grow back."

The good news was the front yard was chock-full of dandelions. The bad news, Melody quickly discovered, was that she had significantly underestimated how stubborn a dandelion root could be. She had already been out in the yard for half an hour when Teeny showed up, and had yet to successfully pull out a single plant with the root still attached.

"I *said*, can I help?" Teeny repeated.

She had scrambled up the fence and was hanging over the top now. Her round face made her plump pink cheeks look like two dinner rolls sitting on a plate.

Melody sighed.

"Maybe your mother needs help with something at *your* house," she hinted.

One of the many annoying things about Teeny Nelson was that she couldn't take a hint. Another was that she asked too many questions.

"How come you're wearing gloves?"

"Because I don't want to get my hands dirty," Melody answered.

"How come your hair's so short?"

"'Cause I like it that way."

"Aren't you scared people will think you're a *boy*?"

"I don't care what people think," Melody said.

Teeny Nelson had on a white tank top with pink lace trim, and her long blond hair was pushed back off her forehead with a sparkly plastic headband. Melody didn't own anything sparkly. She wore jeans in the winter and cutoffs in the summer, sneakers year-round, and on top, either a T-shirt or one of her father's old button-down shirts, untucked with the sleeves rolled up.

Melody jammed the weed fork into the ground beside a large dandelion as Teeny taunted, "I know something you don't know."

"Good for you," Melody told her as she worked the weed fork back and forth to loosen the root.

"Aren't you going to ask me what it is?"

"No."

"It's about *you*," said Teeny, hoping to entice her.

"Still no," said Melody. She couldn't imagine what Teeny Nelson could possibly know that would be of any interest to her.

"Mama says you don't have a mama," Teeny blurted out, unable to hold it in any longer.

Melody snorted.

"You think I don't know that?"

"I'm just saying," said Teeny. "Mama says you don't have one."

Melody set down the weed fork and looked up at Teeny.

"Not that it's any of your beeswax, but my mother died when I was born. So I *did* have a mother, I just don't anymore."

It was not a particularly sensitive subject for Melody. The fact that she didn't have a mother was simply that: a fact. She and her father were very close, and it had always been just the two of them.

"Do you miss your mama?" asked Teeny.

"How could I?" Melody answered. "I never even met her."

"Who cooks dinner for you?"

"My dad."

"Who tucks you in at night?" asked Teeny.

"No one," said Melody. "I'm too old to be tucked in."

"Guess how old I am."

"I don't have to guess. I know how old you are — you're six."

"No I'm not," insisted Teeny. "I'm *going on seven.*"

Melody gathered a handful of leaves and began gently pulling, trying to ease the dandelion plant out of the ground without breaking off the root. No such luck.

"Impudent weed," she muttered, throwing the broken plant down on the lawn, which was already littered with a salad of leaf bits and decapitated yellow dandelion heads. Melody was aware that most ten-year-olds didn't use words like *impudent*, but her father was a high school Humanities teacher. She couldn't help it if she had an unusually large vocabulary for someone her age.

"Why don't you pick the flowers instead of trying to pull out the whole ding-dong thing?" Teeny asked.

Melody didn't feel like having to explain the dos and don'ts of pulling dandelions to a six-year-old.

"Are you sure your mother doesn't need you for something at home?" she asked Teeny.

Teeny crossed her eyes and made a rude noise with her tongue, then let go of the fence and dropped back down into her own yard with a soft thud. Melody heaved a sigh of relief. With Teeny out of her hair, she could turn her full attention to her work. If things didn't pick up soon, she wouldn't be able to afford a single Skittle, let alone two packs of them.

Not long after, Melody's father came out to check on her progress.

"How's it going?" he asked.

"Let's put it this way," she told him. "The dandelions are winning."

Her father laughed. "I'm going to walk down to Wrigley's to pick up a few things," he said. "Want to come along?"

"Absolutely, Boris," said Melody, jumping up and pulling off her gloves.

"As in *positively*, Doris?" her father asked.

"As in *affirmatively*, Boris," she shot back.

"As in *unequivocally*, Doris?"

It was a silly word game they'd invented called Boris and Doris's Thesaurus. Melody quickly racked her brain for another synonym.

"As in . . . *unilaterally*, Boris?" she said uncertainly.

Her father shook his head.

"Nice try, Mel. *Unilaterally* means something done without the agreement or participation of other people it might affect," he said. "Come on — I'll race you to the end of the driveway. Loser has to do the dishes tonight."

Melody was pretty sure her father let her win the race, but she didn't care. Lately he'd been so distracted he burned everything he cooked, and with all the pots and pans that needed extra scrubbing, doing the dishes had become a real chore. And his tendency to burn things wasn't the only unusual thing she'd noticed about his behavior lately. He'd been whistling "You Are My Sunshine" pretty much nonstop for weeks, and just that morning he'd let the bathtub overflow for the second time. More than once Melody had walked into a room and caught him staring off into space with a goofy-looking grin on his face. When she'd asked him what was going on, he'd acted like he had no idea what she was talking about. But Melody knew her father better than anyone. Something was definitely up.

Chapter Two

"Have you ever noticed that most people say 'I could care less,' when what they really mean to say is that they *couldn't* care less?" Melody's father asked as they walked into the grocery store together.

He was always pointing out things like that, which was why, even though she was only ten, Melody knew that it was *champing* at the bit, not *chomping*, and that the expression *the proof is in the pudding* was actually *the proof of the pudding is in the eating*.

"What do you want me to get?" she asked her father.

They always split up the shopping list to save time. There were only a few things on it that day, so while her father headed off to the dairy aisle to get milk and grated cheese, Melody went in search of spaghetti.

"Oh, and we need cereal, too," he called back over his shoulder. "Nothing too sugary, okay, Mel?"

She was reaching for the Raisin Bran when she noticed an eyelash stuck to the tip of her finger. Carefully transferring the eyelash from her fingertip to the back of her left hand, she closed her eyes, made a wish, and blew.

When she opened her eyes, a woman in a tight black dress was strolling by, pushing a shopping cart. She glanced over at Melody and stopped short.

"I'd know that face anywhere!" she exclaimed, and proceeded to march right over and throw her arms around Melody.

Melody had never seen this person before in her life, and was debating whether to punch her in the stomach or scream bloody murder when her father showed up with a gallon jug of 2 percent milk in one hand and a container of Parmesan cheese in the other. The minute the woman caught sight of him, she let go of Melody and threw her arms around him instead.

"There you are, you handsome devil, you!" she cried.

"Here I am," Melody's father said, awkwardly holding the jug of milk out to one side and trying to pat the woman on the back with the hand still clutching the cheese.

"I've missed you, Henry," the woman said, hugging him even tighter.

When she finally let go, Melody's father made the necessary introductions.

"Mel, this is Nancy Montgomery, an old friend of your mother's and mine. Nancy, this is —"

"Melody," the woman said. "I knew it the minute I saw her."

"How do you do," Melody said, extending her right hand, partly to be polite but mostly to make up for the fact that she'd come very close to punching this woman in the stomach a minute ago.

Instead of shaking Melody's hand, Nancy burst into tears.

"You were just a wee little thing the last time I saw you, and look at you now, all grown up and wanting to shake hands."

The way she said it made Melody feel like a dog.

"Even with that short haircut," the woman went on, "I knew who you were. You're the spitting image of your mother."

Melody's father shifted uncomfortably.

"There isn't a day that passes that I don't think about your mother," the woman said, breaking into a fresh round of tears.

"Please, Nancy," Melody's father said quietly.

"I'm sorry." The woman pulled a tissue out of her purse and blew her nose. "She was so young, and I remember how much she was looking forward to having —"

"*Please*, Nancy," Melody's father implored, "this is neither the time nor the place."

As far as Melody could tell, her father *never* felt it was the right time or place to talk about her mother. Melody had once asked him to tell her about the day her mother had died. It was the first time she'd ever seen him cry, and she'd never brought up the subject again. Meanwhile, Melody's father wasn't the only one who avoided talking about her mother. She'd been the closest thing to a celebrity Royal, Indiana, had ever known, but nobody ever mentioned her name anymore — at least not around Melody.

Having recovered her composure, Nancy informed them that the reason she was in town was because her family was having a reunion.

"The theme is *Cherished Moments of Yesteryear*. The name was my idea," she said proudly.

Nancy and Melody's father made small talk for a while. Then, after promising to keep in touch, they said their good-byes, which resulted in more awkward hugging.

"You don't hear that expression very often anymore," Melody's father said later as they left the store with their groceries.

"*Cherished Moments of Yesteryear,* you mean?" asked Melody.

Her father laughed.

"No. *Spitting image.* There's an ongoing debate about its origin. One side claims it was originally *spit and image*; the other insists that *spit* is actually a Southern pronunciation of *spirit.*"

Melody considered asking her father if he thought she looked like her mother too, but decided against it. They had reached the corner, and were standing side by side on the curb waiting to cross the street.

"Why is this light taking so long to change?" Melody complained. "There's hardly even any traffic."

"Patience is a virtue," her father said.

Melody rolled her eyes. "I knew you were going to say that," she told him.

The light changed and they started across.

"So you think I'm predictable, do you?" her father asked. He reached into his pocket and pulled out a pack of Wild Berry Skittles.

"Hey!" Melody exclaimed. "Where did those come from?"

"I had the cashier ring them up when you weren't looking. What do you think of your old man now?"

Melody's father handed her the candy, clearly pleased that he'd been able to pull off the surprise. He, more than anyone, knew how hard it was to keep a secret from her.

"Can I eat them now?" she asked. "I promise it won't spoil my appetite."

"Far be it from me to stand between a girl and her Skittles," he said.

After they got home and had put away the groceries, Melody set the table while her father got dinner started. They were having spaghetti with canned Chef Boyardee meat sauce, one of a grand total of three meals Melody's father knew how to prepare. As he placed the pot of water on the stove to boil, he suddenly remembered something he'd been meaning to ask.

"Did you get your math test back today?"

Melody groaned. "I was hoping you'd forgotten."

Her father opened the drawer and started rummaging around.

"Mel, have you seen the —"

"It's over there," she said, pointing to the can opener, which was in the silverware section of the dish drainer.

"Tell me what happened," he said as he cranked the opener around the metal rim of the can. Chef Boyardee looked on approvingly from the label.

"It was all Miss Hogan's fault," Melody said.

Melody's father was used to hearing her complain about her teacher. Thanks to Miss Hogan, the only positive thing Melody had to say about fifth grade was that it was almost over.

"I got a seventy-three," Melody said as she opened the cupboard and handed him the bottle of olive oil.

He twisted off the cap, poured a few drops into the water, and passed it back.

"Seventy-three?" he said. "How did that happen?"

"'Mary used one cup of sugar to make two cherry pies. How much sugar, on average, did Mary use in each pie?'"

"What was your answer?"

"I said that, on average, Mary used half a cup of sugar in each pie."

Melody's father furrowed his brow.

"Huh. That's what I would have said, too."

"Then you would have been wrong, because the answer is zero point five."

Something sputtered on the stove. Melody grabbed a wooden spoon off the counter and handed it to her father.

"I'm no mathematician, but isn't zero point five the same thing as one-half?" he asked as he lowered the flame and stirred down the sauce.

"Miss Hogan told us all the answers had to be in decimals," Melody explained. "But she didn't use decimals in some of the questions. She was *trying* to trick us."

"Did anybody else fall for it?"

"Nick did," said Melody. "He tried to talk Miss Hogan into changing his grade by telling her that he watches the Food Network all the time and no one ever says *zero point five of a cup* of anything in real life."

"We could use someone like him on the debate team," said Melody's father, his eyes twinkling with amusement.

"You may think it's funny, but I don't. I hate word

problems," said Melody. "And I hate Miss Hogan even more."

"You know how I feel about that word," Melody's father said sternly.

"I know. But Miss Hogan doesn't like me either. She doesn't get any of my jokes and she thinks math is *fun*. I wish I could have had Mrs. McKenna again this year."

Her father nodded. "No doubt about it, you two were a very good fit," he said, rinsing out the empty sauce can and tossing it into the recycling bin. "But I'm sure Miss Hogan has her virtues, too. Did you know that she and Mrs. McKenna are good friends? I always see them sitting together at district staff meetings."

"Really?" asked Melody.

"Ask her yourself," he said. "And while you're at it, why don't you ask her if you can retake the test or do some extra-credit homework to bring up that grade? I'm sure she can be a very nice person if you give her a chance."

Melody suddenly smelled something burning.

"Dad! The sauce!"

The smoke detector started screeching and Melody's father swatted at it with a dish towel until it stopped.

"I'm glad I'm not the one who has to scrub out that pan," said Melody.

"I don't mind," said her father.

He'd been in such a good mood lately; nothing seemed to faze him. As he served up the spaghetti and set the steaming plates on the table he started whistling "You Are My Sunshine" again.

"What is it with you and that song?" asked Melody.

Melody's father reached over and tousled her hair.

"Give me a break. Can't a fellow whistle a happy tune around here if he wants to?" he asked.

But Melody couldn't shake the feeling that her father was hiding something from her.

One way or another, she was determined to find out what it was.

Chapter Three

Honey.

That's what started the whole thing. It's what awakened Melody Bishop in the middle of the night, and what she was still thinking about the next morning when she got up. Maybe she had misheard, she told herself. After all, she had been half-asleep. Or maybe she had dreamed it. But deep down, Melody knew she hadn't been dreaming, and she was certain about what she had heard.

Honey.

It had been a week since she and her father had run into Nancy Montgomery at the grocery store. Her father had continued to behave strangely and deny there was anything unusual going on. As a result, Melody had kept her eyes and ears open, and eventually it had paid off.

After making her bed and tucking her pajamas under the pillow, she got dressed and went downstairs. Her grandfather's oxygen tank was sitting in the hallway, the long thin plastic tube coiled up on the floor beside it, hissing like a snake. Melody had completely forgotten that he was coming to stay for the weekend. She pushed open the screen door and stepped out onto the front porch.

"In case anyone's interested, I'm awake!" she hollered across the yard.

The garage door was open and the scuffed toes of her grandfather's leather slippers were sticking out.

"Be there in a sec!" Gramp-o hollered back. "I'm just looking for the hammer!"

That's what Gramp-o always said when he got caught smoking in the garage. Even after he'd been diagnosed with emphysema, he'd refused to give up his precious Pall Malls. When he thought no one was paying attention, he would unhook himself from his oxygen tank and sneak out for a smoke.

Melody went back inside, where she found a note on the kitchen table scribbled on the back of a yellow flyer announcing the grand opening of a new beauty salon in town. She ran her fingers through her short brown hair. She'd never set foot in a beauty salon. Her grandmother had always trimmed Melody's hair for her when she was little, and after Gram-o had passed away, Melody had learned to do it herself, angling the mirror on the medicine-cabinet door in order to be able to see the back of her head.

Have a great weekend and take good care of Gramp-o, her father had written in his familiar chicken scratch. *In case of emergency call this number.*

Melody sincerely hoped there wouldn't be any reason to call the number since it was impossible to tell her father's eights from his fours or his twos from his threes. He'd signed the note in his usual way, *XO times infinity, Dad.*

Melody set the note aside and poured herself a glass of milk. There was a box of assorted donuts sitting on the table. She chose one dusted with powdered sugar, broke it in half, and was just about to dip it in the milk when the screen door squeaked open and Melody heard her grandfather shuffle in.

"I'm in the kitchen!" she called out to him.

A minute later Melody's grandfather was wrapping his arms around her in a big bear hug. The oxygen tube was back in place under his nose, tethering him to the cylindrical tank, which sat on a little cart beside him. Melody held her breath as she returned her grandfather's hug. She loved him dearly but hated the smell of the cigarette smoke that clung to his clothes and hair.

"Did you see the note from your father?" he asked. "He should have been a doctor with that handwriting of his."

"Do all doctors have bad handwriting?" Melody responded, dunking the tail end of her donut in the milk.

"Mine's got hairy arms," said Gramp-o.

"In case you don't know, that's a non sequitur," Melody told him. "Hairy arms have nothing to do with handwriting. And give me a break, Gramp-o. Do you really think I don't know that 'looking for the hammer' is a euphemism for smoking out in the garage?"

Gramp-o laughed and pinched her cheek.

"Somebody's full of beans this morning," he said. "Any particular reason?"

As a matter of fact, there was.

"Have you noticed Dad's been acting kind of discombobulated lately?" Melody asked.

"Henry's always been a little forgetful, even as a boy, but come to think of it, this morning when I got here I noticed his socks didn't match," said Gramp-o, rubbing his chin.

"That's nothing," Melody told him. "Yesterday I opened the freezer and found a copy of *The Red Badge of Courage* sitting on top of a box of frozen waffles."

"In the freezer?"

"Dad tried to laugh it off, but he's been acting strange for weeks — staring off into space, whistling the same song. And he burns everything he cooks now, too!"

"That reminds me — I made us a tuna noodle casserole for dinner," said Gramp-o.

Melody tried not to let her disappointment show. Her grandfather was a *terrible* cook. She'd been planning to ask if they could order a pizza for dinner.

The phone rang and Gramp-o reached to answer it.

"It's Nick," he said, handing her the receiver a moment later. "I'll give you two some privacy while I go out to the garage to look for — oh, who am I kidding? You're right, it *is* a euphemism."

He started to leave, then paused and put a hand on Melody's shoulder. "Don't worry about your dad, Melly," he said. "He always gets this way at the end of the school year. Once he turns in his final grades, I'm sure he'll be back to his old self again."

What Gramp-o didn't understand was that Melody wasn't worried — she was excited. In fact, she was overjoyed.

As she watched her grandfather head off to the garage, Melody thought back to the previous spring, and the spring before that. It was true that her father tended to get a little distracted at the end of the school year, but this was different. For the past few weeks she'd gotten the distinct impression he was hiding something from her; she was pretty sure now she knew what it was. When she heard a tinny, far-away voice calling her name, Melody realized she'd completely forgotten about Nick.

"*Bishop!*" he was shouting into the phone. "*Bishop, are you there?*"

"I'm here," said Melody. "And you'll never guess what's happened. I'll give you a hint: It's about my dad."

Nick Woo and Melody Bishop had been best friends since they'd been in day care together. People sometimes teased them about being boyfriend and girlfriend, but it wasn't like that at all.

"Don't tell me you found another book in the freezer," Nick said.

"No," said Melody, "but last night, in the middle of

the night, the phone rang and woke me up. I heard my dad talking to someone, then when I asked who had called, he told me it was a wrong number."

"What's so strange about that?" Nick asked. "We get wrong numbers all the time at my house."

"This wasn't a wrong number," said Melody. "My dad definitely knew who she was."

"*She?* How do you know it was a woman?"

"Because right before my dad hung up, I heard him call her something."

"What was it?" asked Nick.

"*Honey.*"

Nick gasped.

"No wonder your dad's been acting so strange," he said. "You know what this means, don't you?"

Melody knew. Even though he'd never said it, Melody could tell her father's heart had been broken when her mother passed away. For years Melody had been making the same wish on every birthday candle, eyelash, wishbone, and shooting star that came her way, and now it had finally come true.

"My dad's got a girlfriend!" she said.

"Who is she?" asked Nick.

That's what Melody wanted to know, too.

Chapter Four

"*Knock-knock!*" Teeny Nelson called through the knot-hole in the fence.

Melody groaned. She was in no mood to be pestered. Her mind was going a million miles an hour trying to figure out who *Honey* was.

"I *said*, 'knock-knock,'" Teeny informed Melody, scrambling up to the top of the fence.

Teeny had on a tight pink T-shirt and her blond hair was pinned up with two silver barrettes decorated with tiny roses.

"I'm busy," Melody told Teeny. "And please don't ask if you can help, because the only thing I need right now is for you to stop bugging me."

Teeny crossed her eyes and stuck out her tongue at Melody, then dropped back down into her yard.

Melody smiled. That had been a lot easier than she'd expected. Returning to her thoughts, she replayed the end of her conversation with Nick in her head.

"I can't stand the suspense. You have to help me figure out who *honey* is!" Melody had told him right before they'd hung up.

"Why don't you just straight-up ask your dad?" Nick had suggested.

"I can't. He went camping, remember?"

"Oh yeah," said Nick. "I forgot about that."

Melody had teased her father mercilessly when he'd first revealed his camping plan. Henry Bishop was not exactly the Boy Scout type, but he was the coach of the debate team, and after winning the statewide championship that year, the members had voted unanimously to reward themselves with a Memorial Day–weekend camping trip. If he didn't get lost in the woods, or eaten alive by mosquitoes, he'd be home around dinnertime on Monday.

Gramp-o had fallen asleep in front of the TV watching CNN and Nick couldn't come over until he'd finished his weekend chores, so Melody decided she might as well take another stab at pulling dandelions while she waited for Nick to arrive. It had rained a little the night before, softening up the ground, and she was finding it a lot easier to work the fork into the lawn. Having loosened a large dandelion plant, she held the jagged green leaves to one side with her left hand and carefully worked the fingers of her right hand down into the dirt until she felt the top of the root through her glove. Wrapping her hand around it, she gave a firm tug. This time the plant popped out of the ground with such force that she fell over backward in a shower of dirt.

"Eureka!" she shouted, holding the dandelion aloft with the hairy brown root still attached.

No sooner had she set her hard-won prize aside and picked up the fork again than one of the fence boards squeaked and swung to the side. Before Melody could say anything, Teeny Nelson squeezed through the gap and stepped into the yard.

What Melody had earlier taken to be a pink T-shirt turned out to be a short-sleeved leotard. Teeny also had on matching tights, which bagged at the ankles, and a little pink tutu that encircled her stout middle. On her feet she wore pink leather ballet slippers held on with narrow bands of elastic.

"Mama got her fingernails painted for free this morning," Teeny announced.

"Fascinating," said Melody, jamming the fork into the ground beside another dandelion and working it back and forth.

Undeterred, Teeny babbled on. "Bee-Bee gave me a root beer Dum Dum and she let me pat her dog, too."

Melody pulled the second dandelion plant out and tossed it on top of the first one.

"Who's Bee-Bee?" she asked.

"She's the tall lady with macaroni hair and orange toenails," said Teeny.

"Thanks," said Melody. "That really helps narrow it down."

Her sarcasm sailed over Teeny's head like a Frisbee.

"Mama says if I'm a good girl, next time I can get *my* fingernails painted, too. Mama got number thirty-two but when it's my turn I'm either going to get number fourteen or number fifty-four."

"Why do the colors have numbers?" asked Melody as she pulled out a third plant and tossed it on the pile. Now that she was getting the hang of it, it was actually kind of satisfying.

"Beats me," said Teeny. "Wanna see me do a trick?"

She reached into the waistband of her tutu and pulled out a yo-yo.

"No thanks," said Melody.

"Wanna see me *pop the clutch*?" asked Teeny.

"No," Melody told her.

"Wanna see me *walk the dog*?"

"Still no."

"*Come on*," Teeny whined, stamping her foot. "Watch me. Watch me do a trick."

"Do you have any idea how annoying you are?" asked Melody. She pulled out a large plant, which actually turned out to be two, bringing her grand total up to five.

"Mama says I can't help it. I was born annoying," Teeny told her.

"That would explain things, all right," said Melody.

Teeny wiped her nose with the back of her hand, then stuck her middle finger through the loop at the end of the yo-yo string and let it drop. It hung for a moment suspended just above the grass, then whizzed back up into her palm with a soft *phwupp*.

"Mrs. Armstrong's mother dropped her teeth down the dispose-all by accident and had to buy a whole new set," Teeny reported, releasing and catching the yo-yo again. *Phwupp*. "And Emily Barber's husband has a piece of bullet stuck in his shinbone."

"Who shot him?" Melody asked.

"Beats me. But Abby Gaebel's appendix burst and

the Lebson family is expecting another visit from the stork."

Phwupp.

"Do you even know what that means?" Melody asked Teeny.

"No. But Wrigley's is having a sale on Miracle Whip and it looks like Henry's been bitten by the love bug."

Melody froze.

"What did you just say?" she asked.

"Wrigley's is having a sale on Miracle Whip."

"No," said Melody. "The other thing."

"It looks like Henry's been bitten by the love bug."

Melody's heart did a little somersault.

"Who told you that?" she asked.

"Beats me," said Teeny. Rising up on her toes, she began to twirl.

"Well, where did you hear it?"

Teeny stopped twirling. Melody could almost hear the gears turning inside her little head. Then a sly smile slid across her face, like butter in a warm pan.

"Give me a turn with that ding-dong fork and I'll tell you where I heard it," Teeny said.

An upstairs window next door banged opened and Mrs. Nelson stuck her head out. Even from a distance

Melody could see that her fingernails were painted a vibrant red.

"Uh-oh," Teeny muttered under her breath.

"Christina Marie!" shouted her mother. "What did I tell you about going into other people's yards?"

"I have to be invited first," Teeny mumbled, kicking at the grass with the toe of one of her pink ballet slippers.

"Excuse me?"

Teeny threw back her head and yelled at the top of her lungs, "I HAVE TO BE INVITED FIRST!"

"Or else?"

"OR ELSE I GET A SPANKING!"

When Melody's father was angry he got very quiet, but he'd never threatened to spank her, let alone actually done it. The miserable look on Teeny's face told a different story.

"It's okay, Mrs. Nelson!" Melody called up to Teeny's mother. "I invited her!"

Teeny was so surprised her eyes looked as if they might pop out of her head and roll around the yard like a couple of hard-boiled eggs.

"Did you hear that, Mama?" she crowed. "I'm *invited!*"

"I heard," said Teeny's mother. "Now get over here, for golly's sake. It's already half past eleven. Roxanne's going to be here any minute to drive you and Julia to ballet, and you know how she hates to wait."

Mrs. Nelson ducked her head back inside and slammed the window shut.

"Well?" said Melody.

"Well what?" asked Teeny.

"Are you going to tell me where you heard that thing about Henry and the love bug or not?"

Teeny considered holding out a little longer for a turn with the weed fork, but they both knew Melody had just saved her from a spanking.

"Okay," said Teeny. "I'll tell you."

The window next door banged open again. By the time Mrs. Nelson stuck her head out, Teeny was already shooting across the yard like a pink comet.

"Wait!" Melody shouted after her. "Tell me where you heard it first."

Teeny had reached the fence. She took hold of the loose board and swung it to the side, but right before she disappeared through the gap, she turned and called back over her shoulder, "At the Bee Hive!"

Chapter Five

Ever since Bee-Bee Churchill was a little girl, putting curlers in her dolls' hair and coloring in their fingernails with markers, she'd dreamed about having her own beauty salon. She even had the name picked out. After high school, Bee-Bee entered the Indiana School of Beauty, quickly rising to the top of her class. She learned how to weave a French braid as tight as a Twizzler, wax an eyebrow without so much as a pinch, and buff a calloused heel smoother than a baby's behind. She could crimp and curl and clip and trim as well as anyone, but the thing that set Bee-Bee Churchill apart from the rest was her uncanny eye for color.

Bored with the humdrum nail polish colors available at the manicure stations at school, she decided to try making her own. Starting with a clear base, she added tiny pinches of powdered eye shadow, patiently mixing the colors until she achieved the exact shade she wanted. For extra sparkle she added a sprinkle of glitter, then dropped two metal ball bearings into the bottle, screwed on the cap, and *clickity-click-click* shook it until the polish was blended and smooth.

"What an extraordinary color!" one of her teachers exclaimed, holding up a bottle of iridescent blue nail polish Bee-Bee had concocted. "I've never seen anything quite like it!"

A proud graduate of the Indiana School of Beauty, Bee-Bee Churchill returned to Cloverhitch to be near her family. She rented a cabin by the river and took a job as a shampoo girl at the only salon in town, Hair Today, Gone Tomorrow. The owner, Devora Flynn, quickly recognized Bee-Bee's gifts and promoted her to head stylist. For the next fourteen years, Bee-Bee saw to the beauty needs of the fine citizens of Cloverhitch. Whether coaxing a reluctant child into the chair for a first haircut or putting the finishing touches on a nervous bride-to-be, Bee-Bee had a way of putting her customers at ease. Her appointment book was always full and her styling chair never empty.

Beauty salons, like churches, are places where people tend to unburden themselves and bare their souls.

Bee-Bee never gossiped herself, but she was a good listener and heard more than her share of confessions over the years. Secrets in a small town are about as easy to keep as a snowball on a radiator, but when it came to Bee-Bee Churchill, even the juiciest of secrets was safe with her.

One day, on a whim, Bee-Bee bought a lottery ticket at the 7-Eleven on the corner of Marion and Main and, against all odds, wound up a winner. After that, everything changed. It wasn't an astronomical sum of money she'd won, but it was enough to make it possible for Bee-Bee to quit her job and begin searching for the perfect spot to open up a salon of her own. There wasn't room enough in Cloverhitch for two beauty salons, so Bee-Bee began contacting real estate agents in neighboring towns and found something that looked promising twenty-five miles east, in Royal.

The Frosty Boy had seen better days, but the minute she laid eyes on it, Bee-Bee knew she had to have it.

Mabel Matthews, the real estate agent who'd arranged to meet Bee-Bee and show her around the place, couldn't have been more pleased.

"Shall we go back to my office and get the paperwork started?" she suggested, eager to strike while the iron was hot.

Bee-Bee hesitated.

"I need to make a phone call first," she said.

Mabel stepped outside to give Bee-Bee some privacy.

The phone call Bee-Bee Churchill made that afternoon lasted only a few minutes, and by the time she hung up the phone, she'd been entrusted with another secret.

"Mabel?" Bee-Bee called out when she was done. "Could you come in here, please?"

Mabel was certain Bee-Bee was about to tell her she'd changed her mind. And why wouldn't she? The place was practically falling down.

"I could show you something else," she told Bee-Bee. "There's a darling little storefront downtown with a partial view of the river and original —"

"I don't need to see anything else," Bee-Bee interrupted. "You can draw up the papers. This is the one for me."

Bee-Bee Churchill's plan was to open her new salon on Memorial Day. There was a lot of work to be done before then, but Bee-Bee could hardly wait to roll up her sleeves and get started. The previous owner had built a cozy little apartment behind the ice-cream parlor. After all the major repairs and renovations had been completed, Bee-Bee and her ten-year-old French bulldog, Mo, moved in and quickly made themselves at home. Every morning at eight o'clock sharp, an army of workers would arrive with tool-boxes in hand, and at five o'clock sharp they would climb back in their trucks and drive away. Bee-Bee worked right alongside them. When they left, she would start dinner and take Mo for a walk. Later, after the dishes had been washed and set to dry, she'd sit down at the kitchen table and make nail polish.

Bee-Bee had decided her salon would feature only homemade polishes. She spent more than she really should have on a beautiful antique glass cabinet to hold them. According to her calculations, it would take exactly one hundred bottles of polish to fill the shelves, and she wanted them all to be ready by opening day.

It had been quite some time since Bee-Bee Churchill had made a polish, and her first few attempts were a bit lackluster, but after a while she got the hang of it again and soon the shelves began to fill with an amazing array of one-of-a-kind colors — deep reds and playful pinks, tropical oranges and luminous blues, greens, yellows, silvers, and golds. Using a mortar and pestle to grind up the powder, she'd place a tiny funnel in the mouth of a bottle and spoon in the colors one at a time. Then she'd add the ball bearings and *clickity-click-click* shake until it was smooth. Night after night, Bee-Bee worked her magic, and when at last she was finished, the nail polish cabinet glowed like a stained-glass window, filling the room with a heavenly light.

Slowly but surely the salon came together. Bee-Bee chose a sunny shade of yellow paint for the outside and installed long wooden flower boxes filled with a medley of pansies, sweet peas, and petunias. Along the front walk she planted honeysuckle and six large snowball hydrangeas, carefully sprinkling coffee grounds and grass clippings around the roots so that the blossoms would turn blue. In lieu of a traditional sign, she commissioned a local artist to carve a giant honeybee, which she hung above the door on a sturdy wire.

Inside the salon, the bee theme continued. The walls were stenciled to look like honeycomb, the styling chairs upholstered in black vinyl with bright yellow stripes, the pedicure tubs were made of golden glass, giant silk flowers hung from the ceiling, strings of tiny lights shaped like bees wound around the base of the pink porcelain shampoo sink, and along the back wall of the salon was a row of dome-shaped hair dryers hand-painted to look like beehives.

Most of the original fixtures from the Frosty Boy had outlived their purpose, but Bee-Bee did keep a few souvenirs — an ice-cream scoop with a wooden handle, a large glass bowl that she scrubbed out and filled with candy to place on the counter beside the cash register, and an old photograph which the previous owner had left behind. It was the first thing Bee-Bee had seen when she'd walked through the door of the Frosty Boy with Mabel Matthews, and she had taken it as a sign that she was meant to be there.

A week before the opening, Bee-Bee sent out flyers printed on bright yellow paper, offering a free manicure to anyone who stopped by the salon before noon. Then she crossed her fingers and waited for the big day to arrive.

On Saturday morning of Memorial Day weekend, Bee-Bee woke up early. After a light breakfast of ginger tea and wheat toast, she got dressed, put a dab of vanilla behind each ear (she preferred it to perfume), and took Mo for a long walk to calm her nerves. By the time they returned, a line of customers was already forming outside the salon. Bee-Bee was so happy she practically jumped for joy.

"Welcome!" she cried as she hurried up the steps to greet them. "Welcome to the Bee Hive."

Chapter Six

Mo had no memory of his mother. His eyes were barely open when she was taken away. The runt of the litter, he felt small and insignificant in comparison to his older brothers and sisters. Food at the puppy mill was scarce, and with all those hungry mouths to feed, more often than not, Mo went to bed without supper. He wasn't much to look at, with his bowlegs and bony chest.

One day Mo was out in the yard, watching two of his brothers play tug-of-war with a ratty old dish towel, when a shiny new white car rolled up the driveway. A thin man with glasses and a large woman in a yellow dress got out of the car, carefully picking their way around the piles of melting slush until they were standing next to the chain-link fence.

The large woman rested one hand on her belly and shielded her eyes from the sun with the other, searching. After a moment she pointed to Mo.

"That's him," she said. "That's the one."

The next thing he knew, Mo was sitting in the backseat of the white car. The thin man with glasses kept glancing in the rearview mirror at Mo and the large woman was singing, *You are my sunshine, my only sunshine . . .* in a high clear voice as they sped down the road toward a new chapter in Mo's life.

When they arrived at the big house, Mo could hardly believe his good fortune. For the first time in his life he had more than enough to eat, a soft bed to sleep in, toys to play with, and every day from dawn till dusk the house was filled with beautiful music. The thin man with glasses was nice in a quiet way, but the large woman quickly became Mo's favorite. She smelled like lilies of the valley and delighted in spoiling Mo with treats, fussing over him like a mother hen. Mo finally knew what it felt like to be loved. He filled out and grew stronger, and thanks to the large woman's patience and gentle reminders, learned to mind his manners and do as he was told.

One day the large woman surprised Mo with a

41

gift, a heart-shaped silver pendant with his name engraved on it. "You're a good boy," she said as she fastened the chain around his neck. Mo was so excited he raced around the room wagging his stubby little tail until it was nothing but a blur. He loved the way the pendant jingle-jangled when he moved and the way it made him feel like he belonged. What would his brothers and sisters think of him now? How envious they would be of his wonderful life!

Mo loved his new life, and hoped it would never change, but one morning in mid-March, he awoke to a strange sound coming from upstairs. High-pitched and urgent, it hurt Mo's ears and set his teeth on edge.

No one came downstairs to give him breakfast, and soon the house began to fill with strangers. The hurried clicking of their heels on the steps frightened Mo. He took refuge in the back room, curling up on the blue velvet couch to wait for everyone to leave. There was no music that day. Dinnertime came and went, and when the last of the strangers had finally left, Mo crept upstairs to the bedroom. The large woman was asleep, her hair spread out on the white pillow behind her like a halo. Beside her on the bed lay a small bundle wrapped in gray cloth.

An unfamiliar odor lingered in the air, something damp and fresh, like new-cut grass. In the corner of the room, near a window, stood the thin man, his head bowed, his shoulders slumped. Behind the lenses of his glasses, his eyes were like two bottomless black holes. When he saw Mo, his face crumpled and he began to cry.

"Go away," he told Mo. "Please, just go away."

The next morning the thin man with glasses came downstairs to give Mo his breakfast, something he had never done before. The man didn't warm up Mo's food the way the large woman always did — he dumped the can straight into the dish, and he forgot to fill the water bowl and give Mo his vitamin. A few hours later, the man went out, carrying the gray bundle in his arms. As soon as he was gone, Mo went looking for the large woman. He searched the house from top to bottom, but she was nowhere to be found.

That afternoon, more strangers came to the house, all of them dressed in black. Among them was a tall woman with a kind face and a soft voice. She smelled like sugar cookies and there was something about her manner that immediately put Mo at ease. She was the last of the strangers to leave that day, and before she did, she knelt down beside Mo and spoke to him gently.

"Don't worry, Mo," she told him. "Everything's going to be okay. You're going to come live with me for a little while. Won't that be nice?"

The tall woman took Mo home with her. That night she fed him leftover chicken and dumplings and lit a fire in the potbelly stove to help take the chill out of the air. Mo curled up on the couch in front of the stove but he couldn't sleep. He was grateful for the tall woman's kindness, and the delicious chicken and dumplings, but he couldn't stop thinking about the big house and the wonderful life he had left behind. Where had the large woman gone? Didn't she love him anymore?

Right before Mo had left, the thin man with glasses had bent down and patted him on the head.

"Just for a little while," he'd said as he undid the clasp and slipped the silver chain from around Mo's neck.

Now Mo missed the jingle-jangle sound and the way it made him feel. Like he belonged.

Exhausted, he finally closed his eyes. As the fire crackled in the potbelly stove and the moon hung like a shiny gold pocket watch in the sky, he had the dream for the first time.

The image of a girl danced behind his eyelids. Sunlight caught in her long yellow hair, and when she threw back her head and laughed, Mo's breath quickened and his heart began to race. The girl stopped laughing and looked at him with wide eyes. "It's you," she whispered. Then she ran to him, threw her arms around his neck, and Mo followed her home. This was where he belonged. Where he was meant to be. With her. If only he knew who she was.

Chapter Seven

Things were really hopping at the Bee Hive. By ten o'clock there was a line of customers stretching half-way around the block. Everyone made a big fuss over the décor, and there was much oohing and ahhing over the selection of homemade nail polish colors — the one-hundredth bottle of which Bee-Bee had finished mixing at midnight the night before.

Her customers were in good spirits, laughing and chatting with each other as Bee-Bee flew around the salon flitting from hand to hand, soaking, filing, clipping, buffing, and painting fingernails. That morning, she gave manicures to the mayor's wife, the pharmacist's sister, a pair of identical twins, and the church organists from both the Methodist and the

Presbyterian churches. Even the elderly widow of the former owner of the Frosty Boy stopped in to have her nails done. She recognized the glass bowl sitting on the counter right away.

"George used to keep his sprinkles in that, back in the day," she said wistfully as she plucked a bottle of ruby-red polish off the shelf and held it up to the light. "Of course I remember that, too," she added, pointing to the old photograph Bee-Bee had rescued from the Frosty Boy and hung on the wall behind the shampoo sink. "Once upon a time that little girl was quite famous, you know."

The happy chattering of her clientele reminded Bee-Bee of the flocks of catbirds that used to come to feed in her mulberry trees back in Cloverhitch. She worked steadily, humming softly to herself. By noon she had managed to give thirty-six manicures to a total of thirty-five satisfied customers.

The lone discontent had been Teeny Nelson's mother. Mrs. Nelson had frowned at her fingernails when Bee-Bee was finished painting them and complained that the color had looked different in the bottle. Bee-Bee quickly apologized and offered to start fresh with a new color, even though there were other customers waiting. Then she told Teeny to help herself to a piece of candy from the glass bowl on the counter and asked if she'd like to go say hello to the dog while her mother got her nails repainted.

"Does he bite?" Teeny had asked, digging around in the candy.

Bee-Bee shook her head.

"He's a perfect gentleman," she told Teeny. "Unless you happen to be a cat. Go right down that hall and through the white door. My guess is you'll find him napping on the couch."

By noon the rush was over. Bee-Bee scribbled *out to lunch* on a piece of paper and taped it to the front door, then went back to the apartment to make herself a bite to eat.

Having finally finished his chores, Nick Woo arrived at the Bishops' house just in time for lunch.

"I thought you'd never get here," said Melody as she let him inside.

Gramp-o slapped together a couple of baloney-and-cheese sandwiches and poured Melody and Nick each a glass of milk.

"I've got some errands to do in town this afternoon, Melly," Gramp-o said. Then he frowned and snapped his fingers. "Darn. I just remembered I left the tuna noodle casserole in the trunk of my car — would you mind bringing it in? The keys are on the hook by the door."

"I'll come with you," said Nick.

As they walked across the lawn to the driveway, where Esmeralda, Gramp-o's banged-up old white car, was parked, Melody filled Nick in on what Teeny had told her.

"I'm telling you, it's not a coincidence," she insisted as she popped open the trunk. "Teeny Nelson was talking about my dad — *he's* the Henry who's been bitten by the love bug, and somebody at the Bee Hive knows about it."

Melody lifted the large Tupperware container out of the trunk. Gramp-o had made enough tuna noodle casserole to feed an army. They'd be eating leftovers for weeks.

"Is it my imagination or is that new?" Nick asked, pointing to a dent in the rear bumper.

Grampo's driving was about on a par with his cooking.

"He backed into a fire hydrant last week," Melody explained as she slammed the trunk closed. "It came 'out of nowhere' like everything else he's hit."

"What does your grandfather have to say about what's going on with your dad?" asked Nick.

"He doesn't get it," said Melody. "He thinks the reason my dad's been acting weird is because it's the end of the school year. But I've already started a list of potential *honey*s. I have to know who she is."

"Maybe your dad told your grandfather about his new girlfriend, but he swore him to secrecy or something," said Nick.

That hadn't occurred to Melody. On their way back inside, she decided it couldn't hurt to ask.

"Thanks," Gramp-o said when Melody set the heavy container on the counter, "I'll take it from here. But first I'm going out to the garage."

"To look for the hammer?" asked Nick.

Gramp-o shook his head.

"Don't you get started with me, young man," he said, unhooking the oxygen tube and draping it over the back of a chair.

"Before you go," said Melody, "can I ask you something?"

"Fire away," Gramp-o told her.

"Has Dad mentioned anything to you about having a girlfriend?"

Melody studied her grandfather's face carefully as

he answered. She'd played enough games of gin rummy with him to know that his eyebrows twitched when he was being shifty about something.

"If your father has a girlfriend, it's news to me," Gramp-o said, his eyebrows unmoving. "What makes you think he might?"

"All the signs are there," Nick chimed in.

"You said yourself you noticed Dad's socks didn't match," Melody pointed out.

Gramp-o laughed. "This from the person who gave *me* grief about a non sequitur? Listen, Melly — I'd like your father to find someone special as much as you would, but if he was seeing somebody, he would have told us. Mark my words, the minute he's done with school, he'll straighten up and fly right again."

"Like I said," Melody told Nick after her grandfather had left. "He doesn't get it."

She got a bottle of chocolate syrup out of the fridge, and put a generous squirt in her glass. Then she tilted her head back and squirted a long stream of chocolate directly into her mouth.

"Jenny would kill me if she saw me do that," said Nick.

Jenny was Nick's stepmother.

"You want some?" Melody asked Nick.

He nodded and held out his glass.

"Where is this Bee Hive place anyway?" he asked.

The name had rung a bell as soon as Teeny had said it. Melody had seen the advertisement for the grand opening on the yellow flyer her father had written his note on the back of.

"It's where the old Frosty Boy used to be," she told Nick. "As soon as we're done eating, I think we should go over there and snoop around a little."

Nick hesitated. "I've never been to a beauty parlor before," he said.

"Neither have I," admitted Melody. "But all we're going to do is go in, ask a few questions, and get out."

"What if someone tries to paint my fingernails or something?" Nick asked.

"Don't worry," Melody assured him. "I'll protect you."

They carried their milk and sandwiches out onto the front porch.

"You know what I've been thinking about lately?" asked Nick, sitting down next to Melody on the top step. "Water towers."

"What about them?" Melody had always been rather fond of the shiny metal mushroom-shaped tower that stood on the edge of town. She especially liked the way it had *Welcome to Royal* written across the top in loopy blue script.

"Every town around here has one, but how do we know for sure there's water inside?" asked Nick.

"Why would anyone bother to build a water tower if they weren't going to put water inside it?" asked Melody.

"Good question," said Nick. "Another thing I'd like to know is why they need to have all those antennas and blinking lights on top."

Melody took a bite of her sandwich and licked a drip of mustard off her thumb.

"Why don't you Google it?" she asked.

"I've Googled it, Binged it, and Asked Jeeves. They all say the same thing, but I'm not convinced."

"What do you mean?" asked Melody.

"What if it's some kind of a plot? What if these so-called water towers are actually full of alien creatures with see-through brains and huge boogity eyeballs, sending messages back and forth because they're planning to take over the world?"

"Have you completely lost it, Woo?" Melody laughed. "You sound certifiable."

"Go ahead and mock me if you want," Nick told her. "But don't blame me when you're lying in your bed some night and a slimy green tentacle dripping with ectoplasmic ooze comes slipping through your window and grabs you by the neck."

"Can we please stop talking about aliens and get back to the subject of my father's new girlfriend?" asked Melody.

"Maybe *honey* is an alien," said Nick. "Did you ever think of that?"

"Only you would think of that. Besides, I doubt my dad would fall for someone with boogity eyeballs and a see-through brain."

Nick gulped down half of his chocolate milk, and wiped his mouth on his sleeve.

"What did the person look like who said the thing about Henry and the love bug?" he asked, peeling the crust off one half of his sandwich and popping it in his mouth.

"Teeny doesn't remember who said it, but whoever it was knows my dad," Melody said.

Nick wasn't so sure.

"Henry is a pretty common name," he said. "How do you know they weren't talking about some other guy?"

"Did you bring your phone?" Melody asked.

She didn't have a cell phone. Neither did her father. In fact, they didn't even have a home computer.

Henry Bishop had strong feelings about screen time. Melody wasn't allowed to watch TV at all on weekdays, and she only got two hours of viewing time on weekends.

"I'm starved," said Nick, through a mouthful of bologna and cheese. "Can it wait until after we finish eating?"

One look at Melody's face told him the answer.

Nick set down his sandwich, reached into his back pocket, and pulled out his phone. Tapping in the search information, he waited. Nick loved his phone. When he first got it he'd spent hours trying out different names for the built-in electronic "personal assistant" to call him. Finally he settled on "Your Majesty."

Nick typed in a few searches, then turned to Melody, satisfied.

"You'll be happy to know that according to this, there's only one Henry in Royal, Indiana," he told her, "and it's your dad. Now all we have to do is track down the love bug who bit him."

Chapter Eight

Mo was sitting on the living room rug, scratching an itch behind his left ear. That morning, after a long walk, the tall woman had brought him home. After filling Mo's bowl with fresh water, she'd given him a rawhide knot and left, closing the door behind her. There were strangers around, all women. They clucked and cackled like a bunch of chickens, but at least they were quieter than the men who'd been showing up every day for weeks with their noisy tools. All that pounding and buzzing had made Mo want to throw back his head and howl.

When he and the tall woman had lived in the cabin beside the river, life had been more peaceful. The only sounds Mo heard were the birds singing and the wind in the trees at night. He had enjoyed chasing grasshoppers and rolling in the patch of sweet clover near his favorite shade tree. He'd spent many happy hours burying soup bones under that tree. By now the dopey old beagle down the road had probably come and dug them all up. The tall woman seemed happier since the move; she hummed all the time, but Mo hadn't made up his mind yet about the new place. He felt nervous and on edge all the time now. As if something were about to happen. But what?

It didn't help matters that there was a cat hanging around. Mo heard him yowling in the middle of the night, and even though Mo barked whenever the big orange cat showed himself, the cat had still left his musky scent all over the yard. Mo hated the smell of cat even more than he hated getting a bath. Fortunately, the tall woman had been too busy lately to think about bathing Mo, or clipping his nails — another thing he hated. Mo would be vigilant. Eventually the cat would get cocky, the way cats always did, and Mo would chase him up a tree and show him who was boss.

Mo chewed on the rawhide knot for a while, and when he grew tired of that, he curled up on the couch to take a nap. He had just closed his eyes when he heard someone open the door. The step was unfamiliar, lighter and quicker than the tall woman's. A minute later, a little girl peeked around the corner. She had long yellow hair, and when she tipped back her head and laughed, Mo's breath quickened and his heart began to race. It was her! The girl from his dream!

Mo knew what was going to happen next: She would run to him and throw her arms around his neck. But instead, to his surprise, the girl skipped across the room and patted him gingerly on the head. Her fingers were sticky and smelled of root beer, and she was shorter and rounder than she was supposed to be. She laughed again, then turned and skipped away. Mo didn't bother to follow. She wasn't his girl. She wasn't his girl at all.

Chapter Nine

"See?" said Melody excitedly. "I told you it wasn't a coincidence. The Henry that Teeny was talking about was definitely my dad."

A car horn beeped and Nick and Melody looked up to see Roxanne Jenkins sailing by in a red SUV. Julia Jenkins and Teeny Nelson were buckled up next to each other in the backseat, on their way home from ballet class. Melody waved and Roxanne waved back.

"Maybe she's *honey*," Nick suggested.

"I already put her on the list," Melody told him. "You remember the pound cake, right?"

When Melody was a little girl, Roxanne and her husband had split up. One day she'd showed up on the Bishops' doorstep with a homemade pound cake and a lot of eye makeup on. Later Melody's father had explained that Roxanne had come on a fishing expedition.

"What was she trying to catch, Daddy?" Melody had asked.

"Me, I suppose," he'd said.

"Do you want her to catch you?"

"No," Melody's father had told her. "I don't."

"I do," Melody had said, licking her lips. "That pound cake was delicious."

Now Melody and Nick watched the red SUV turn the corner and disappear behind a row of hedges.

"Who else is on your list?" asked Nick.

"That woman, Nancy, I told you about, who hugged my dad in the grocery store, and Miss Berg."

"The lady at the library who wears those funny red glasses?" asked Nick incredulously.

"Love is blind," Melody told him.

"Lucky for Miss Berg," he said.

"Can you think of anyone else we could add to the list?" asked Melody.

"What about my neighbor Bethany Mitchell?" said Nick. "She's not married and there's definitely nothing wrong with the way she looks."

"She might look okay, but have you ever heard

her talk?" Melody asked. "She says *suppose-ably* and *anyways*." Her father would never be interested in someone who spoke that way.

"I still think you should add her to the list," said Nick.

Melody sighed. "Fine. She's in the running."

"Maybe your dad met *honey* on one of those dating websites. That's how my dad and Jenny got together."

Nick's parents had gotten divorced when he and Melody were in second grade, and his dad had remarried a year later. Nick loved Jenny, and Melody thought she was great, too — and not just because she made good chocolate-chip cookies.

"I tried to talk my dad into doing online dating once," Melody told Nick. "I even came up with a screen name for him, Word Nerd, but he refused to try it."

"Why do you think your dad hasn't told you he's seeing somebody?" asked Nick, flicking a crumb off his knee.

"I don't know. But I'm sure he has a reason. He never does anything without thinking it through first."

Nick stood up.

"Speaking of food," he said, "I could use another sandwich."

"Who was speaking of food?" asked Melody.

"Oh," said Nick, "I guess I was just thinking about it."

"Well, stop thinking about it," said Melody, grabbing Nick's hand and pulling him down the steps. "We have some detective work to do!"

It was about a ten-minute bike ride from the Bishops' house to the Bee Hive.

As they pedaled past the high school, Melody happened to glance over at Nick and noticed he was chewing on his bottom lip.

"What's the matter?" she asked.

"Nothing," he said.

"Hello? This is your best friend talking. You think I don't know what it means when you chew on your lip? What's wrong?"

"It's just, well, I think I might have come up with a theory about why your dad doesn't want to tell you who he's been seeing, but I warn you, you're not going to like it."

"I promise not to shoot the messenger," Melody said.

"What does *that* mean?"

"It means you should tell me your theory, and I won't blame you if I don't like it."

"Okay," said Nick. "Here goes. Maybe the reason your dad doesn't want you to know who he's seeing is because he's afraid you won't be happy about it."

"I've been wanting this forever," said Melody. "Why wouldn't I be happy about it?"

"What if *honey* is someone your dad knows you don't like. I mean, really, really, *really* don't like."

"Like who, for instance?" asked Melody.

"Nobody in particular," said Nick. "It's just a theory."

Melody shook her head. "I don't buy it. If I don't like someone, he probably wouldn't like them either."

"Yeah. You're probably right. Like I said, it was just a theory."

They had come to a steep hill, so they got off their bikes and started walking them up.

"Do you want to stay for dinner tonight?" Melody asked.

"Sure," Nick said.

"You may regret that decision when you taste Gramp-o's tuna noodle casserole. It's truly vile."

"I'm just glad to be here. I almost got grounded this weekend."

"Why?" asked Melody.

"Why do you think?"

"Oh, because of the math test?" Melody guessed.

"It wasn't our fault we got so many wrong," he said as they got back on their bikes. "Miss Hogan deliberately tried to trick us. I wish we could have had Mrs. McKenna again this year."

"I told my dad the exact same thing."

"Remember when Mrs. McKenna took us to the museum to see that dinosaur?" asked Nick.

Melody nodded. *"Dracorex hogwartsia."*

She still had the picture of Nick and her posing in front of the skeleton with their arms draped around each other's shoulders. It was pinned to the bulletin board that hung above the desk in her room.

"That was the coolest thing ever," Nick said.

"No," Melody corrected, *"Mrs. McKenna* was the coolest thing ever. My dad told me that she and Miss Hogan are friends."

"No way!" shouted Nick.

"Miss Hogan is the opposite of Mrs. McKenna," said Melody. "She doesn't think anything is funny. On the rare occasions when she actually smiles, she looks like she's in pain, and Miss Hogan definitely wouldn't have done something amazing like take the whole class to the Indianapolis Children's Museum to see a sixty-six-million-year-old dinosaur named after something from Harry Potter."

"You can say that again," Nick agreed.

As they glided around the corner side by side on their bikes, the Bee Hive came into view.

"Holy moly!" exclaimed Nick. "Check out the big bee!"

But Melody wasn't looking at the bee. She was looking at a woman in a navy-blue wraparound dress who was walking up the sidewalk in their direction. She couldn't quite put her finger on it, but there was something very familiar about her. She had on a straw sun hat with a wide floppy brim, so Melody wasn't able to see her whole face, but she could tell by the way the woman was pursing her lips that she was whistling. As she got closer, Melody caught a snippet of the tune.

"You are my sunshine, my only sunshine . . ."

"Who is that?" Melody asked Nick.

They both watched as the woman in the straw hat crossed the street and headed up the front walk to the Bee Hive. Just before she opened the door, she paused and took off her hat.

Melody gasped.

"Speak of the devil," said Nick. "It's Miss Hogan!"

Chapter Ten

Melody was beside herself.

"Calm down," Nick told her. "You're jumping to conclusions."

"Think about it." Melody started ticking off the evidence on her fingers. "Miss Hogan's not married, she lives here in Royal, she's someone my dad knows I really, really, *really* don't like, and she was whistling the same song he's been whistling every day for the past month. *How do you explain that?*"

"A lot of people know that song," Nick said, trying to reassure his friend. "And like I told you before, that thing I said about your dad was just a theory. He's a nice guy — why would he ever want to go out with someone like Miss Hogan?"

"You mean someone who has no sense of humor, who enjoys tricking her students, and has permanent lipstick stains on her front teeth?"

"Basically," said Nick. "Plus, I don't know whether you've ever noticed this, but her earlobes are freakishly large."

"Is this actually happening?" asked Melody. "What if my dad and Miss Hogan get married? What if she and her freakishly large earlobes come to live with us in our house? I'll have to move to Siberia!"

"I'm telling you, Bishop, you're jumping to conclusions," said Nick.

He started to wheel his bike across the street.

"Where are you going?" asked Melody.

"I thought you wanted to snoop around."

"What's the point? We already know who *honey* is."

Nick continued across the street, but instead of going up the front walk in plain view, he went around to the side. Leaning his bike against the yellow wall, he sneaked over to one of the windows and peered in. After a minute he gestured for Melody to come join him.

"Fine," she grumbled. "But I'm *not* going inside."

Melody leaned her bike against the wall next to Nick's and joined him at the window.

"I see Miss Hogan," whispered Nick, pressing his nose against the glass. "She's talking to some tall lady with curly red hair."

"That must be Bee-Bee," Melody told him, remembering Teeny's description of her macaroni hair.

Noticing the window was open a crack, Nick slipped his fingers under the edge and slowly inched it up. He and Melody leaned closer.

"I was thrilled when I heard you were opening up a beauty salon," they heard Miss Hogan saying. "Your timing couldn't be better."

"I'm glad to hear that," said Bee-Bee as she led Miss Hogan over to one of the black-and-yellow-striped styling chairs. "So what are we doing today? Manicure? Pedicure?"

"Actually, what I need is some advice," Miss Hogan said. "About hair. I can't decide whether I should wear it up or down. Then of course there's the question of ornamentation. I was leaning toward mother-of-pearl combs, but now I'm worried it might be too much."

"This is boring," whispered Nick.

"*Shhh*," Melody shushed him.

"The first thing I'll need to know is what kind of occasion it is," said Bee-Bee.

"I can't tell you that," said Miss Hogan. "It's a secret."

"Can you at least tell me if it's black tie or casual?" asked Bee-Bee.

Melody noticed Miss Hogan seemed flustered.

"I really don't know the details yet," she said. "It's all rather sudden. We haven't even told our families. I suppose everyone will know about it soon enough anyway, so I might as well just tell you — I'm getting married!"

Melody felt like she'd been punched in the stomach. If Miss Hogan was getting married, that meant —

"Knock-knock."

Someone tapped Melody on the shoulder from behind. Startled, she spun around to find Teeny Nelson standing there in her tutu.

"Go away!" Melody hissed, waving her away from the window.

"You're not the boss of me," said Teeny, folding her arms over her chest.

Melody grabbed Teeny by the elastic waistband at the front of her tutu and dragged her over to where her neon-pink bike was parked on the sidewalk.

"What are you doing here?" Melody demanded.

"Did you find out about Henry and the love bug yet?" asked Teeny.

"That's none of your business," snapped Melody.

"It is so," said Teeny. "You wouldn't even know about it if I hadn't told you."

Nick came over and joined them.

"Are you okay, Bishop?" he asked, putting his hand on Melody's arm. "Your face is kinda red."

"Is he your boyfriend?" asked Teeny, pointing at Nick.

"No," Nick and Melody said at the same time.

"Do you have a suntan or are you always that color?" Teeny asked Nick.

Nick's mother was African American and his father was Chinese.

"What kind of question is that?" snapped Melody.

"I'm just saying," grumbled Teeny.

"Does your mother know you're here?"

Teeny looked down at her pink ballet slippers, which were streaked with dirt and grease from her bicycle chain.

"Maybe," she said. "Or maybe she had a headache and told me to watch TV for an hour while she lay down and took a nap, for golly's sake."

"You didn't come all the way here by yourself, did you?" Nick asked.

"I wore my helmet," Teeny told him, pointing to

the Styrofoam Dora the Explorer bike helmet hanging from the handlebars of her bike. "And I didn't cross until I saw the white walky man light up."

"You're too little to be riding around by yourself," said Melody. "Besides, you don't belong here. This isn't some silly game we're playing. This is about my life, or what's left of it, anyway."

"I want a Dum Dum," said Teeny.

"How can you think about candy at a time like this?" asked Melody.

"I want a Dum Dum," Teeny said again.

She started toward the door but Melody reached out, snagging her by the back of her tutu this time.

"Not so fast," she said.

"I want a Dum Dum!" insisted Teeny, trying to wriggle free.

"You're not going inside," Melody told her. "None of us are."

Teeny turned around and glared at Melody.

"Why'd you come all the ding-dong way here if you're not even going to go inside?" she asked. "Don't you want to know about Henry and the love bug anymore?"

"No," said Melody.

"*But I want a Dum Dum,*" Teeny whined.

"Are you sure you don't want to go inside?" Nick asked Melody. "I still think you might be wrong about Miss Hogan."

"How much more proof do you need?" she asked him. "She's *honey*, and not only that, apparently she's marrying my dad."

Teeny, still fixated on getting a Dum Dum, decided it was time to take matters into her own hands.

"I'm going in!" she announced.

There was a loud ripping sound and Teeny took off running, leaving Melody standing there with her mouth hanging open and what was left of Teeny's pink tutu in her hand.

Chapter Eleven

"That little miscreant," fumed Melody as she balled up the torn tutu and shoved it into the basket on the front of Teeny's bike.

"What do we do now?" asked Nick. "We can't just leave her here."

He was right, of course, but Melody was furious at Teeny for barging in. As if she didn't have enough to deal with already.

"Come on," she told Nick. "I suppose we'd better see what Teeny is up to."

Nick followed her back to the window.

"There she is," said Nick, cupping his hands around his eyes and peering into the salon.

They watched as Teeny, in only her leotard and

tights, skipped across the salon and tugged on Bee-Bee's sleeve. Bee-Bee stopped what she was doing and leaned down, listening. Then she nodded her head and pointed to a glass bowl sitting on the counter. Teeny skipped over to the bowl and, after pawing around for what seemed like about an hour, finally found what she was looking for.

Melody preferred Blow Pops and Tootsie Pops to Dum Dums, but now that Teeny had her precious sucker, Melody hoped she would turn around and come back outside so they could leave. Instead, Teeny tugged on Bee-Bee's sleeve again, then, to Melody's dismay, she pointed toward the window. Melody grabbed Nick and they ducked down as quickly as they could, but it was too late.

They'd been spotted.

"Come on in and join the party, you two," Bee-Bee called out from the doorway a minute later. "The more the merrier."

"Now what are we going to do?" asked Melody.

Nick shrugged. "What choice do we have?"

"But what are we going to say if Miss Hogan asks us what we're doing here?"

"Don't worry," Nick assured her. "I'll think of something."

• • •

"Welcome to the Bee Hive," Bee-Bee said, holding the door open as Nick and Melody reluctantly entered the salon.

Teeny had been right — Bee-Bee Churchill's hair *did* look like macaroni, and it was a shade of red that could only have come from a bottle. Now that she was standing beside her, Melody realized Bee-Bee had to be close to six feet tall. She was wearing a flowery dress and leather sandals, revealing ten long pale toes, each nail painted a beautiful pinkish-orange color that reminded Melody of ripe papaya.

"Do I know you?" Bee-Bee asked Melody. "Your face looks familiar."

"Her name's Melody and she doesn't have a mama," said Teeny, who was elbow deep in the candy bowl again.

Bee-Bee put her hand to her mouth and Melody wasn't sure, but she thought she saw tears in her eyes.

"You're Melody?" she asked.

Do you know me? Melody thought to herself. *Am I supposed to know you?*

"*Melody Bishop?*" Miss Hogan cried, jumping up out

of her chair. "And is that Nick Woo with you? What on earth are you two doing here?"

"Hello, Miss Hogan," Melody muttered.

"What are you doing here?" Miss Hogan asked again.

Melody turned to Nick, since he'd promised that he would handle this question if it came up — but Nick was busy gawking at the flowers on the ceiling and wasn't paying attention.

"I know why they're here," Teeny piped up. "They want to know about Henry and the love bug."

"Henry and the who?" asked Bee-Bee, confused.

"Ignore her," Melody said quickly. "She doesn't know what she's talking about."

"Do so," Teeny insisted. Then she stuck her tongue out at Melody and ran over to one of the black-and-yellow-striped styling chairs. Throwing herself into it headfirst, she began pushing off the floor with her feet to make it spin.

"Look at me!" she squealed.

"I'm waiting," Miss Hogan said, looking at Melody expectantly.

Melody jabbed Nick in the ribs with her elbow to get his attention.

"Miss Hogan wants to know why we're here," she said. "I thought maybe you'd like to tell her."

"Oh," said Nick, clearly caught off guard. "So you want to know why we're here?"

"I believe I've made that abundantly clear," said Miss Hogan.

In the pressure of the moment, Nick panicked and blurted out the only thing he could think of:

"We came to get our fingernails painted!"

"Yippee!" shouted Teeny, leaping out of the chair. "I want to pick my color!"

Dizzy from spinning, Teeny careened across the room toward the cabinet containing the bottles of Bee-Bee's homemade nail polish. But as she wobbled and weaved past Melody, somehow Teeny got tangled up in her own feet and went flying, knocking the glass candy bowl off the counter and sending it tumbling to the floor with a terrible crash.

Chapter Twelve

Mo didn't usually have dreams during the day, only at night, but that afternoon after his encounter with the little girl with the sticky fingers, he fell asleep on the couch and his eyelids immediately began to twitch. There she was again. His girl. The sunlight caught in her long yellow hair, then she threw back her head and laughed — but wait. What was this? Something new, or had he simply not noticed it before? The girl was holding something in her right hand, her fingers clasped tightly around it. *"It's you,"* she whispered, and started to open her hand. Mo caught a glimpse of something shiny . . . but then a terrible crash suddenly woke him from the dream before he could see what was in her hand.

Chapter Thirteen

"It wasn't my fault!" Teeny wailed. "Melody pushed me!"

"I didn't push you, Teeny," Melody insisted.

"Did so!"

"Stop arguing and somebody go find a broom," Miss Hogan said, taking charge.

"There's one over there in the corner," Bee-Bee said, pointing. "I'll go get the dustpan. Everyone, please be careful not to step on the glass."

"I'm gonna pick out my color," said Teeny. Then she turned to Nick and added, "I'll pick one out for you, too, if you want."

"Uh, that's okay," said Nick.

Teeny marched over to the glass cabinet and, after examining the bottles of nail polish for a minute, plucked number fifty-four from the shelf. Teeny looked over her shoulder to see if anyone was watching. There was something she'd been itching to do since the minute she'd walked into the Bee Hive. With everyone busy cleaning up the glass from the broken bowl, now seemed like the perfect time. Moving slowly, so as not to draw attention to herself, she made her way across the room to the row of hair dryers. Quietly climbing into a chair, she pulled one of the dome-shaped beehives down over her head and switched it on, grinning happily as the hot air began to whip her hair around.

"We're really sorry," Nick told Bee-Bee as he took the dustpan from her and squatted down on the floor.

"No worries," Bee-Bee told him. "I'm just glad nobody was hurt."

Miss Hogan swept a pile of broken glass and candy into the dustpan, then turned to Melody.

"What do you have to say for yourself?" she asked.

"What do you mean?" Melody replied.

"The child says you pushed her."

"I didn't," said Melody. But she could tell by the look on her face that Miss Hogan didn't believe her.

"If there's one thing I can't abide in a person" — Miss Hogan sniffed with disdain — "it's dishonesty."

Melody felt her face getting hot. She knew she shouldn't say anything, but she couldn't help it.

"That's pretty funny coming from you, don't you think?" she said.

Miss Hogan's eyes flashed, and when her upper lip curled, Melody saw a bright red lipstick stain on her front teeth.

"I'm sure I don't know what you mean," Miss Hogan snapped.

"You don't have to pretend anymore, Miss Hogan," said Melody. "Your secret is out. I know about the wedding. I know about *everything*."

Miss Hogan was mad as a hornet.

"You ought to be ashamed of yourself, Melody Bishop, poking your nose into other people's business! How dare you? When your father gets back from his camping trip, the three of us are going to sit down and have a serious talk about this."

Your father. The way she said it was so . . . familiar. It gave Melody chills.

After thanking Bee-Bee for her time, Miss Hogan snatched up her hat and stormed out of the Bee Hive, slamming the door behind her.

Melody turned to Nick.

"Now do you believe me?" she asked miserably.

There was no getting around it — things did not look good. Miss Hogan hadn't denied anything, and the fact that she knew Melody's father had gone camping was pretty incriminating, too.

"I'm sorry, Bishop," Nick said. "Is there anything I can do?"

"Yeah. Ask your phone to find out how much a one-way ticket to Siberia costs," she told him. She was only half kidding.

Bee-Bee, who had been standing there quietly through all of this, finally spoke up.

"Can somebody please explain what just happened?" she asked.

"It's kind of a long story," Nick told her. "But I guess we should start by telling you that we didn't really come here to get our fingernails painted."

"I did!" cried Teeny. She had grown bored with the hair dryer, and was ready to move on to the main event. Her hair was so tangled and teased up from being under the dryer, she looked like a tumbleweed with pink legs. "Here's the color I want," she said, holding up the bottle of nail polish she'd chosen earlier.

Melody glanced over at Nick. "Do you want to tell her, or should I?"

When Teeny found out she wasn't going to be getting a manicure after all, she had a total meltdown.

"It's not fair!" she said, stamping her foot. "I already picked out my color!"

"Maybe you can come back some other time with your mother," Bee-Bee suggested.

"But I want to do it *right now!*" Teeny sobbed, throwing herself down on the floor in despair.

"Is there anything else you can think of that might cheer you up?" Bee-Bee asked, leaning over her.

Teeny looked up at Bee-Bee, and Melody could hear those little gears turning inside her head again.

"Candy makes my feelings feel better," Teeny sniffled.

It might have been the first thing Teeny had ever said that Melody agreed with. But a mountain of Wild Berry Skittles wouldn't have cheered Melody up now.

Bee-Bee went to the supply closet, where she kept her stash of candy, and came back a minute later holding a bouquet of Dum Dums in her hand.

"What flavor do you want?" she asked.

"Root beer," said Teeny, plucking a sucker from the bunch. "And mystery, too," she added, helping herself to a second Dum Dum, this one with yellow question marks decorating the wrapper.

"What flavor is mystery?" asked Nick.

"Mystery flavor," said Teeny, pulling off the wrapper and jamming the Dum Dum into her mouth.

"We should get going," said Melody. "Teeny's mother might be worried."

"Mama's taking a nap," said Teeny. "And I want to go in the back and see the dog."

"This isn't a good time," said Bee-Bee quickly.

"I just want to pat his head!"

"The answer is no," said Melody firmly. "Undeniably, indisputably, categorically *no*. It's time for us to go."

Teeny glowered at Melody, then turned and started to make a run for the white door that led to Bee-Bee's apartment. Only Nick was too quick for her. He scooped her up and tossed her over his shoulder like a wriggling pink sack of potatoes.

"Come on, short stuff," he said. "We're outta here."

Nick carried Teeny outside, but when Melody reached the door, Bee-Bee put a hand out to stop her.

"I wish you'd stay," she told Melody. "Just for a little while. We need to talk."

"If it's about the bowl," said Melody, "I'm sure my dad will lend me the money to buy you a new one."

"It's not about the bowl," said Bee-Bee.

"Bishop!" Nick called from outside. "Are you coming?"

"Please stay," said Bee-Bee.

Melody hesitated, then leaned out the door.

"Would you mind taking Teeny home?" she asked Nick. "I'll meet you back at the house in a little while."

He didn't question her. He just nodded. From the way Teeny was looking at him, Melody knew she'd be no trouble at all on the ride home. It was impossible not to like Nick Woo.

Once they were off, Melody closed the door.

"Thank you," said Bee-Bee. Melody noticed her eyes looked moist again.

"So what did you want to talk to me about?" Melody asked.

"Your mother," Bee-Bee said.

Chapter Fourteen

"Did you know my mother?" asked Melody.

Bee-Bee nodded. "We were best friends back in elementary school."

"Do you know my dad, too?" Melody asked. "His name is Henry Bishop."

"I met Henry for the first time at your mother's funeral," said Bee-Bee. "That's where I met you, too."

"Was I there?" asked Melody, surprised.

"Sleeping in your father's arms," said Bee-Bee. "Surely he must have told you about it."

"He doesn't like to talk about my mother very much," said Melody. "Nobody does. I think they're afraid it might make me sad."

A dog barked and Bee-Bee jumped as if she'd been poked with a stick.

"Is that your dog?" asked Melody.

"Yes," said Bee-Bee. "He's probably spotted a cat."

The dog barked again and Bee-Bee jumped even higher.

"Are you okay?" Melody asked.

"I'm fine," said Bee-Bee, smoothing a wrinkle from the front of her dress. "Just a little tired."

"I should probably get going," Melody told Bee-Bee. "Nick's waiting for me."

"Before you go, I want to show you something."

Bee-Bee walked over to the shampoo sink and took the framed photograph off the hook. Melody had been so busy contending with Miss Hogan, she hadn't even noticed it hanging there.

It was a faded *Time* magazine cover. On it was a picture of a girl with long yellow braids sitting on a piano stool in a pair of overalls, blowing a big pink bubble with her gum. The headline read, *Hoosier Wunderkind*.

The cover story had been about a girl named Annabelle Winters who'd started playing the piano at the age of three. Before she'd lost her baby teeth, she was giving concerts with some of the most renowned symphony orchestras in the world. Audiences went wild over the little girl from the Midwest who could play Tchaikovsky and Rachmaninoff as easily as "Chopsticks."

What the magazine article didn't mention was that after her time in the spotlight, Annabelle stopped giving concerts and went home to Royal, Indiana, where she became a piano teacher and eventually got married and started a family. Annabelle Winters had been America's darling and the pride and joy of Royal. She had also been Melody's mother.

"This is the Annabelle I remember," said Bee-Bee. "After this picture was taken, your mother's career began to take off. Then my family moved west to Cloverhitch, and Annabelle and I lost touch."

"That's too bad," said Melody. She was having a hard time imagining her mother as a little girl in elementary school with long yellow braids and a best friend.

"You look just like her, you know," said Bee-Bee.

It was the second time in a week someone had told her that. Melody studied the photograph carefully, but she couldn't see any resemblance between her and this beautiful girl with the long yellow braids.

"You can keep it if you want," said Bee-Bee.

"Thanks," Melody told her. "But my father might not like that. He probably wouldn't want any reminders of my mother lying around, now that he and Miss Hogan are getting married."

"What?" said Bee-Bee.

"That's the whole reason Nick and I came here today. Teeny Nelson heard somebody talking about Henry being bitten by the love bug when she was here this morning with her mother."

"I don't remember hearing anything like that," said Bee-Bee. "Then again, things were a little crazy around here this morning."

"It doesn't matter anymore," said Melody. "I knew my dad was seeing somebody — I just didn't know who she was. Now I do."

"I gather you're not too fond of Miss Hogan," said Bee-Bee.

Melody shook her head sadly. "Can I ask you something?" she said. "What was my mother like?"

Bee-Bee smiled and put her hand on Melody's shoulder.

"Why don't we go sit down?" she said.

Bee-Bee led Melody over to a wicker bench under one of the windows and they sat down next to each other.

"I only knew Annabelle when she was younger," Bee-Bee began. "But I doubt she changed very much. Everybody always wanted to be around her. She was smart and pretty and funny —"

"She was funny?" asked Melody. The few times her father had talked about her mother, he was so sad and somber. It never occurred to Melody that her mother could have been *funny*. She'd always pictured her as this serious person who could play the piano in front of huge audiences without even getting nervous. Not some funny little girl who chewed Bazooka and knew how to crack a joke.

Bee-Bee nodded. "I remember she used to do these impressions of her mother that were so accurate it was almost scary."

Melody wasn't close to her maternal grandparents. Omi and Opa had moved back to Switzerland not long after Melody was born. They sent her a card on her birthday each year, but other than that, she had very little contact with them.

They had disappeared, too.

Now Melody felt something she hadn't let herself feel before. Left behind.

"What else do you remember about my mother?" she asked Bee-Bee.

"The same thing everyone else remembers: She was unbelievably talented. When she sat down at the piano, she'd get this faraway look on her face. And when she started playing — well, have you ever heard her play? There were lots of recordings made."

Melody shook her head. There were boxes of tapes and CDs on the shelves in the music room, but the door to that room was always kept closed. It wasn't that Melody wasn't allowed to go in; she'd just never had any real desire to.

Melody cleared her throat. There was a question she had been wanting to ask for a very long time. A question her father had made clear he didn't want to answer.

"How did my mother die?"

Bee-Bee hesitated. Obviously Melody's father was not comfortable talking to Melody about her mother, and it sounded as if he must have communicated this somehow to the people around her, too. Bee-Bee didn't want to go against his wishes. But on the other hand, it was clear Melody was looking for answers to some very important questions.

"I don't know the details," Bee-Bee said, "other than that it was sudden and unexpected. Your mother had wanted a home birth, but there were complications. That's really all I know."

Melody was quiet. Deep down inside her something was stirring, a feeling she couldn't quite find the right words to describe.

"Will you tell me about the funeral?" she asked.

Bee-Bee reached over and took Melody's hand.

Her fingernails were painted a pale shade of pink that reminded Melody of the inside of the conch shell Gramp-o had brought back for her from a trip he and Gram-o had taken to Florida.

"There were lots of people there," Bee-Bee began, "but nobody spoke a word. There was no minister, and no speeches were made. There was only music."

"What kind of music?" Melody asked.

"If I remember correctly, it was a string quartet. Wonderful musicians your mother had played with when she was younger. Then, at the end, your dad played a tape he'd made of your mother playing one of her favorite pieces. He'd recorded it himself at home, not long before you were born. You could hear Annabelle laughing and talking about —" Bee-Bee started to get choked up and had to stop for a minute. "It was a lovely memorial. Lovely, just like Annabelle was."

Melody felt tears prickle up in her eyes and the mysterious feeling got stronger.

"Miss Hogan isn't lovely," she said. "And she isn't funny either. Why would my dad want to marry someone like that?"

"I don't know," said Bee-Bee, shaking her head.

"Neither do I," Melody told her. "I wanted him

to find someone special, but I thought she'd be more like —"

"Your mom?" said Bee-Bee.

"No. *Me.*"

A single tear rolled down Melody's cheek, and she brushed it away.

"Don't worry, Melody," Bee-Bee said, squeezing her hand. "Everything's going to be okay."

How Melody wanted to believe her — but she didn't see how it could possibly be true.

Chapter Fifteen

Mo felt uneasy. The large orange cat had been lurking around outside all day. He'd barked at him earlier, and he had run under a bush, but Mo could tell he was still nearby. The tall woman would be back soon, to give him his supper. After that, she would probably sit at the kitchen table and *clickity-click-click* until it was time to go to bed. Lately she'd been too busy to spend much time cooking. He couldn't even remember the last time she'd made him chicken and dumplings or a nice roast. Instead she'd been giving him kibble with a few table scraps tossed in. He hoped she hadn't grown tired of him, and that she wouldn't disappear into thin air, the way the large woman had. Even though it had happened a long time ago, he still remembered her and the silver necklace she'd given him. How he'd loved the way the jingle-jangle made him feel.

Mo looked out the window. The cat was nowhere to be seen. He thought about chicken and dumplings. The tall woman always made sure to give him plenty of gravy. And she was careful to remove the bones first before she filled his dish. Chicken bones could splinter and get stuck going down. Mo thought about roast beef. The tall woman always saved the end piece for him. Crispy and dripping with juice, he would barely take the time to chew, he was so eager to gobble it down. Mo's stomach rumbled. What would he be having for supper that night? He wondered. Whatever it was, he hoped there would be a lot of it. He lifted his nose and caught a whiff of new-cut grass. Then he went and sat by the door to wait for the tall woman to come home.

Chapter Sixteen

Since Melody wouldn't accept the photograph, Bee-Bee tried to give her a bottle of nail polish instead.

"I'm not really a nail polish kind of person," Melody explained. "As you can probably tell. Don't get me wrong — I think the colors you make are really beautiful. This yellow one reminds me of a daffodil, and this blue one looks like a swimming pool, and the one you've got on your toes is the exact color of a ripe papaya."

"I wish you would come up with names for all of my polishes," said Bee-Bee, impressed.

"Why do you put numbers on them, anyway?" asked Melody.

"I'm not clever with words, the way you are," Bee-Bee told her.

Melody held up a bottle of dark blue polish. Bits of glitter caught in the light and made it sparkle like a thousand stars. If they were real stars, Melody would have made the same wish on every one of them, but wishing was what had gotten her in trouble in the first place.

"I should get going," Melody said, putting the bottle of polish back on the shelf. "Nick must be wondering where I am."

The phone started to ring.

"I'd better get that," Bee-Bee said. "It might be a customer. Please come back and see me again soon. My door is always open if you want to talk."

As Melody left, she heard Bee-Bee pick up the phone.

"It's a beautiful day at the Bee Hive!" she sang into the receiver.

But it didn't feel like a beautiful day to Melody. It felt more like the end of the world.

When Melody got home, Nick was waiting for her on the front steps with a bag of Skittles in his hand.

"They were out of Wild Berry, so I got you Original," he said.

Melody thanked him for the Skittles and immediately tore open the pack.

"How did it go with Teeny?" she asked, tossing a handful of candy in her mouth. Wild Berry or not, they still tasted good.

"Luckily for her, her mom was still asleep when we got there. But Teeny's going to have some explaining to do about the state of that tutu."

"Do you still want to stay for dinner?" asked Melody. She offered him some Skittles, but Nick shook his head.

"I kind of figured dinner was off. I'm sure you don't exactly feel like celebrating."

"Believe me," said Melody, "eating Gramp-o's tuna noodle casserole is no party."

Nick laughed. He was relieved to hear Melody making a joke.

"You know," he said, "if your dad and Miss Hogan actually do get married, you don't have to go to Siberia. You can come live with me. We've got a spare room in the basement, and my dad and Jenny are crazy about you."

"Tell the truth," said Melody, tossing another handful of candy into her mouth. "If things had gone differently at the Bee Hive today, and we'd actually had to get our fingernails painted, would you have gone through with it?"

"Absolutely," said Nick. "But only if I got to pick my own color."

Melody smiled. She was lucky to have a friend like Nick.

It would be several hours before it was time for dinner, so Melody asked Nick if he'd like to help her dig up some dandelions.

"My dad said he'd pay me a nickel for each one," she explained. "If we make enough, maybe we can buy a new bowl for Bee-Bee."

"That's a great idea," said Nick.

They found a second weed fork in the garage and got down to business.

Nick turned out to be pretty good at pulling dandelions. Meanwhile, Melody came up with a new strategy, picturing Miss Hogan's face on every plant she yanked out.

It was very effective.

"Bee-Bee was pretty nice, didn't you think?" asked Nick.

"Yeah," said Melody.

"She sure does like bright colors," said Nick, loosening the dirt around another plant. "Good thing she's not a dog."

Melody stopped what she was doing and looked at him.

"Okay," she said, "I'll bite. Why is it a good thing that Bee-Bee isn't a dog?"

"Because dogs are color-blind. They can only see yellow and blue — everything else looks gray."

"How do you know that?"

"Mrs. McKenna told me last year. Remember all those stories she used to tell us about her dog, Oreo?"

"His name was Mallomar," said Melody.

"I knew it was a cookie," said Nick.

By the time Gramp-o called them in for supper, Nick and Melody had amassed an impressive pile of dandelions, all with the roots still attached.

"If you want, I can come back tomorrow and help you pull more," Nick offered.

As soon as they sat down at the table, Nick and Gramp-o started arguing about who the top draft pick for the Pacers ought to be. Melody liked basketball, but she had more important things on her mind. She couldn't stop thinking about her father and Miss Hogan.

"What's the matter, Melly?" Gramp-o asked after a while. "Don't you like my casserole?"

"I'm not very hungry," she said, pushing a slimy noodle across the plate with her fork. "I'll just drink my milk."

Nick, who was always hungry, cleaned his plate in two seconds flat and asked for more.

"What did the two of you do this afternoon?" asked Gramp-o, dropping a heaping spoonful of tuna noodle casserole onto Nick's plate.

Nick glanced at Melody.

"Not much," he said, shoving another forkful of noodles into his mouth.

Melody had asked him not to discuss their trip to the Bee Hive with Gramp-o. When her father got home on Monday, she planned to tell him what had happened with Miss Hogan. He could give Gramp-o the big news about the wedding himself.

After dinner, Nick and Melody helped clear the table and load the dishwasher, then Gramp-o looked at the clock and asked if they'd like to watch *Jeopardy!* with him.

"It doesn't count as screen time because it's educational," Gramp-o insisted.

"Way to circumvent, Gramp-o," laughed Melody. He often let Melody stretch the rules when he was around.

Melody popped up a bag of microwave kettle corn, and she and Nick joined Gramp-o in the den to watch *Jeopardy!* One of the categories in the first round was American Classics.

"What is the Grand Canyon?" Gramp-o called out in response to a clue. "No, wait, I take that back. What is American cheese?"

It was during Final Jeopardy that Nick started rubbing his stomach.

"I don't feel so good," he said.

"Me neither," said Gramp-o.

What followed was not pretty. It turned out that Melody was lucky to have lost her appetite at dinner. The tuna noodle casserole, having sat in the hot trunk of Gramp-o's car for hours, wasn't in the best condition, and as a result both Gramp-o and Nick got food poisoning. Nick had to call his father to come pick him up, and Gramp-o retreated to the upstairs bathroom, where he would revisit that casserole many times before the night was over.

It had been a long and difficult day. Melody was exhausted, but the sound of Gramp-o dragging his oxygen tank back and forth to the bathroom was too much for her to take, so she decided she might be better off finding somewhere else to sleep. Nick had thrown up on the couch in the den right before he left, and the pullout sofa bed in her father's office was covered with books and papers. This left only one option, so, grabbing her blanket and pillow, Melody went downstairs to the music room.

She had never slept there before. In fact, she couldn't even remember the last time she'd gone in. There was something sad about the way the room felt, like a party after the guests have gone home and all that's left is a bunch of empty cups and crumpled napkins. Tall sets of shelves crammed with books and boxes lined the walls, and in the corner of the room sat her mother's piano, the lid closed and the glossy black surface dulled by a layer of fine dust. Gram-o had taught Melody how to play "Chopsticks" on the piano when she was a little girl, but that was the extent of her repertoire, and it had been ages since she'd played even that. There was a faded blue velvet couch along the back wall. Melody spread out her blanket, switched off the light, and settled herself in.

As she lay there in the dark, going over the events of the day in her head, she remembered how, when Teeny was having her meltdown, Bee-Bee had asked if there was anything she could do to help Teeny feel better.

"Candy makes my feelings feel better," Teeny had told her.

Melody wished the solution could be that easy for her now. She had enjoyed the Skittles Nick had brought her, but candy couldn't even begin to touch the misery she felt inside. The only thing she could think of that would make her feel better was if she woke up the next morning and found out this whole thing had been a bad dream.

If only that could really happen, Melody thought as she turned over and closed her eyes. *If only, if only, if only . . .*

Chapter Seventeen

Sunday morning when Melody woke up, the sky was an ominous gray and raindrops were pelting the windowpanes like spitballs. She went upstairs to check on her grandfather, but found his door closed. Pressing her ear against the wood, she could hear him snoring. Poor Gramp-o. It must have been a long night, but at least he was resting now.

Melody poured herself a bowl of Raisin Bran. She thought about calling Nick, but decided it might be best to wait until later. Chances were he'd had a rough night, too.

After she'd finished her breakfast, Melody returned to the music room to retrieve her pillow and blanket. As she was leaving, something caught her eye. It was a small black tape recorder, lying on its side on one of the shelves. Melody picked it up, flipped open the lid, and found a tape inside. The yellowed label was peeling off around the edges. On it, in her father's handwriting, it said, *Brahms Intermezzo, Op.117-1* and then the day and the year. Exactly two days before Melody was born.

There was a rumble of thunder. The rain was coming down harder now. Melody set the tape recorder on top of the piano and pushed PLAY. When nothing happened, she used her fingernail to pry open the little slot on the side and discovered four badly corroded triple-As inside. After a fruitless search of all the logical places in the house a fresh battery might be, Melody suddenly remembered there was a tape player in Gramp-o's car.

She fetched an umbrella from the hall closet, grabbed the keys off the hook by the door, and, still in her pajamas, ran barefoot out to the car. Lightning flashed as she yanked open the heavy door and slid into the driver's seat. Melody had never driven a car, of course, but Gramp-o had once showed her how to start it. After checking to make sure the arrow on the gearshift was pointing to *P* for park, she inserted the key and turned it gently to the right. Nothing.

She vaguely remembered Gramp-o saying something about giving it a little gas. Since she wasn't sure which of the two pedals was the gas, she put one foot on each of them and pressed down hard, then turned the key again. This time the engine caught and Esmeralda roared to life, sending up a billowing cloud of exhaust behind her.

There was a tape already in the player — *The Best of the Beach Boys*. Gramp-o loved the Beach Boys. Melody ejected it and slipped in the tape she'd found in the music room, then she pressed PLAY.

There was a soft hiss, then a creak, and then the music began. A piano, playing slowly at first, until the melody began to swoop and swell. Melody shivered. It was cold in the car, so she turned on the heater. Then she leaned her head back and closed her eyes. She never listened to classical music, but she could have sworn she'd heard this piece before — so many times, in fact, she knew every note by heart. *How is that possible?* she wondered. As the music wrapped itself around her, Melody wanted to curl up inside the sound and float there, safe and warm forever. When it was over, and the last sweet note had faded away, she heard a woman's laughter, and then her voice.

"Turn that silly thing off and come feel this, Henry," she said. *"I think our baby likes Brahms. She's kicking like a little kangaroo."*

Melody recognized the sound of her father's laugh joining in.

Then the tape softly clicked off.

Silence.

Melody listened to the tape twice more. Just as she was about to rewind it to listen for a fourth time, someone knocked on the car window. Startled, Melody turned to the left, and there was Mrs. McKenna, standing out in the rain.

"Melody!" she shouted. "Is everything okay? Open the window."

Melody quickly rolled down the window.

"Are you okay?" Mrs. McKenna asked again. "I was driving by and saw you sitting in the car alone and got worried."

There was another flash of lightning, followed by a loud boom of thunder that made them both jump. Mrs. McKenna drew her collar tight around her throat, ran around to the other side of the car, and climbed in.

"What are you doing out here all by yourself, sweetie?" she asked.

Melody felt numb.

"Gramp-o's inside," she said. "Asleep. He and Nick got sick last night and my dad's away for the weekend."

"You scared me half to death," said Mrs. McKenna, putting her hand over her heart. "I thought something awful had happened."

Melody started to shake as the mysterious feeling that had been hiding deep down inside her finally rose up to the surface, bubbling and boiling until she couldn't hold it back any longer and it spilled out over the edges of her heart.

"Poor thing," said Mrs. McKenna, taking her into her arms. "Tell me what's wrong."

Melody dug down deep and finally found the words to describe what it was she'd been feeling.

"I miss my mother," she sobbed.

"Of course you do, sweetie," said Mrs. McKenna, rocking her gently. "Of course you do."

Melody and Mrs. McKenna sat together out in the car for a long time. After a while, the rain began to let up and they turned off the engine and went inside the house to check on Gramp-o. While Melody headed upstairs to see if he needed anything, Mrs. McKenna went into the kitchen to make a pot of tea.

"Gramp-o says to please forgive him, but he's not feeling up to saying hello," Melody reported when she came back downstairs. "And he asked me to look around and see if we have any saltines."

"What he needs is Vernors ginger ale," said Mrs. McKenna. "I can pick some up for him at Wrigley's on my way back from the Bee Hive."

"Are you going to the Bee Hive?" asked Melody.

Mrs. McKenna nodded. "I'm treating myself to a manicure."

"Nick and I were there yesterday," said Melody.

Mrs. McKenna lowered her eyes.

"Yes, I heard," she said.

Melody remembered what her father had said about Mrs. McKenna and Miss Hogan being friends.

"If Miss Hogan told you that I pushed Teeny, she was flat-out lying," said Melody. "She doesn't like me, you know."

"Don't be silly," said Mrs. McKenna. "Miss Hogan was just upset about her secret getting out. As secrets go, it's a pretty big one."

"Tell me about it," Melody grumbled.

Mrs. McKenna looked at her watch.

"My appointment is at eleven," she said. "I hate to leave you here alone. If you feel up to it, why don't you join me? I'll treat you to a manicure — I hear the colors are out of this world."

The teakettle began to whistle on the stove, and Mrs. McKenna went and turned it off. Melody watched her move around the kitchen, making the tea. She seemed so at home. When she was finished, she found some saltines in the pantry, made a little fan out of them on a plate, and asked Melody to take the tea and crackers up to her grandfather.

"Tell him I hope he feels better," she said. "And ask him if it's okay for you to come with me to the Bee Hive."

"Will you be mad if I decide not to get my finger-nails painted?" asked Melody.

"I won't be mad," Mrs. McKenna promised. "But when you see how much fun it is, you might change your mind."

Two days ago Melody had never set foot in a beauty salon in her life, and now she was going for the second day in a row.

"Let's go, Kokomo," said Mrs. McKenna, slipping her raincoat on.

"Kokomo?" asked Melody.

Mrs. McKenna laughed. "It's something my husband always used to say."

"Is he from Kokomo, Indiana?"

"No — he just liked the way it sounded."

Melody did, too. Her dad had been right when he'd said that she and Mrs. McKenna were a good fit. It was so easy to be around her. Melody made herself a promise: She was not going to think about anything sad for the rest of the day. Instead she was going to enjoy her time with Mrs. McKenna and maybe, just maybe, get her fingernails painted, too.

Chapter Eighteen

Mo hated the rain and he hated thunder and lightning even more. That morning the tall woman practically had to drag him out the door to get him to take his walk. Once he was outside, Mo did his business as quickly as possible, then he whined pitifully until the tall woman had no choice but to turn around and take him home.

"What a big baby you are," she teased.

The ground was muddy, and Mo stepped carefully around the puddles. He didn't want to get his feet dirty. The last thing he wanted was to give the tall woman a reason to give him a bath. She insisted on using the same shampoo on him that she used on herself. It was okay for her to smell like peppermint candy, but Mo preferred smelling like himself. A dog's sense of smell is a powerful thing, and Mo's nose was particularly sensitive. He could tell when the milk was about to turn, and if there were mice nesting in a wall. He'd smelled the rain coming long before the first drop fell. Mo lifted his head. His nose was picking up another smell now. Something very close.

They had just started up the front walk when the orange cat came scooting out from under a bush. Mo saw his chance. He jerked so hard on the leash, the tall woman lost hold of it, and Mo took off after the cat like a shot. After chasing him around in circles for a while, the cat finally ran up a tree, at which point the tall woman caught up with Mo and took hold of his leash again.

"First you act like a baby," she scolded him, "then you turn around and start acting like a bully. Shame on you, Mo."

Back inside, she dried Mo off with a towel and, in spite of what he had just done to the cat, gave him a rawhide knot to chew on. Then she put fresh water in his bowl, closed the door, and left.

Mo curled up on the couch to take a nap. He was pleased with himself for having treed the cat. The rain had stopped and there was even a hint of sun peeking through the clouds. He closed his eyes, hoping that the dream would come. *"It's you,"* the girl would whisper, and Mo would follow her home. The night before he had waited for the girl, wanting to see what she was holding in her hand, but she hadn't come.

Maybe it was just a chew toy she had in her hand. Maybe it was a soup bone, or a biscuit.

Or maybe it was something more than that.

Mo was certain that it was something more, but he couldn't really say why.

Sometimes a dog just knows.

Chapter Nineteen

"What happened to your hair!?" Melody exclaimed.

Bee-Bee's curls were gone, replaced by a jet-black bob with bangs.

"I like my hair to match my mood," she told Melody. "Come on in, I'll show you my collection."

Melody quickly introduced Mrs. McKenna to Bee-Bee and they both followed her into the salon.

"Voilà!" said Bee-Bee, opening a closet door to reveal several shelves filled with Styrofoam heads wearing wigs of every color and style imaginable, including the red macaroni curls she'd had on the day before.

"What fun!" said Mrs. McKenna. "Can you imagine what my fourth graders would think if I came to school wearing one of these?"

"I have you down for a manicure today, is that right?" Bee-Bee asked, leading them back out into the main room.

Mrs. McKenna nodded. "I'm trying to talk Melody into having one, too — but she's still on the fence."

"Why don't I get you started, and Melody can decide later on," said Bee-Bee. "First pick a color."

Mrs. McKenna walked over to the glass cabinet to look at the polishes.

"These are exquisite," she told Bee-Bee.

"I'm hoping Melody will help me name them."

"She's got a way with words," said Mrs. McKenna, "that's for sure. What are you going to call this silvery one, Melody?"

Mrs. McKenna held up a bottle of sparkly polish. It was the very first polish Bee-Bee had made for the salon.

"Hmmmm," said Melody. "Maybe Silver Linings?"

Bee-Bee whistled.

"You're good!" she said.

"What about this one?" asked Mrs. McKenna, holding up another bottle.

The first thing that popped into Melody's head was Lipstick Stain, because the polish was the same shade as the lipstick stains on Miss Hogan's front teeth. But Melody had promised herself she wasn't going to be gloomy, so she quickly came up with a more cheerful name for the bright red polish in Mrs. McKenna's hand.

"Candy Apple."

"You're hired!" cried Bee-Bee. "Seriously, I've got some labels in the drawer by the phone, and there's a black sharpie in there, too. Knock yourself out."

Mrs. McKenna selected a beautiful coral polish with swirls of gold running through it, and while Bee-Bee got to work with her emery board and cuticle nippers, Melody sat cross-legged on the floor nearby making up polish names and writing them carefully on the labels.

"Where does the inspiration for your colors come from?" Mrs. McKenna asked Bee-Bee. She was soaking her fingertips in a bowl of warm water with rose petals floating in it.

"Close your eyes," Bee-Bee told her, "and tell me what you see."

Mrs. McKenna closed her eyes.

"What am I supposed to be looking for?" she asked.

"Colors," said Bee-Bee. "Every feeling has them. Whenever I sit down to make a polish, the first thing I do is close my eyes and take a minute to get in touch with my feelings. That's where all my ideas come from."

"I see mostly yellow," said Mrs. McKenna, "with a little bit of orange around the edges. Also some tiny pink stars."

"You must be feeling happy today," said Bee-Bee. "Pink, yellow, and orange are all happy colors. When you're feeling sad, you see blues and greens."

Melody closed her eyes, too.

"What does it mean if you see red?" she asked.

"Red is a tricky one," Bee-Bee told her. "It can either mean passion or heartache."

There was an awkward silence. Everyone in the room knew which of those feelings Melody had been experiencing lately.

"I have a funny story to tell you," Mrs. McKenna jumped in, breaking the silence. "I have this little boy in my class, Jacob, who was doing a report on Booker T. Washington for Black History Month. What do you remember about Booker T. Washington, Melody?"

"The *T* stands for Taliaferro and he was one of the most influential African American leaders in America from 1895 until his death in 1915."

"That was impressive," said Bee-Bee.

Melody shrugged. "I did my report on him, too," she explained.

"So, anyway," Mrs. McKenna went on, "poor Jacob made the mistake of running a spell check without proofreading afterward and ended up with a report about an esteemed African American statesman named *Booger* T. Washington instead of *Booker*."

Melody giggled. "Remember last year when the lady from that peace organization came to talk to us about Mahatma Gandhi?" she reminded Mrs. McKenna. "She wanted us to make up a list of questions we would ask if we were sitting next to him at a dinner party. Nick said he would want to ask Gandhi if he had any pets. You and that lady laughed so hard you both cried."

"I miss Nick Woo," said Mrs. McKenna. "How is he doing?"

"Fine," said Melody. "Except that he's obsessed with water towers."

"I have a thing about water towers, too," said Bee-Bee. "There's something so friendly-looking about them, you know?"

"Yeah, well, Nick thinks they're full of boogity-eyed aliens dripping with ectoplasmic ooze."

"Ectoplasmic Ooze. Now *there's* a nail polish name for you," said Bee-Bee.

They all laughed at that. Then Melody got back to work. By the time Bee-Bee had finished painting Mrs. McKenna's nails, Melody was almost done naming the polishes.

"What about it, Melody?" Bee-Bee asked. "Manicure for you today, too?"

"I don't think so," she replied. "Maybe some other time. I have to come back anyway, to finish naming the colors."

"Sounds good," said Bee-Bee. "And when that time comes — we'll mix up a special color together just for you. Number one hundred and one."

"What will you call it, Melody?" asked Mrs. McKenna.

"I'm not sure. I'll have to think about it."

Melody was sad to leave the Bee Hive that afternoon, and sadder still to have to say good-bye to Mrs. McKenna when she dropped her off. They had stopped at Wrigley's on the way to pick up a bottle of Vernors for her grandfather.

"I guess I'll see you around," said Melody, tucking the ginger ale under her arm and opening the car door.

"Take care, Melody," said Mrs. McKenna.

As Melody watched her drive away, the sad feeling started to bubble up inside her again. She'd been keeping a lid on it all day. It had been so wonderful spending time at the Bee Hive, making up names for Bee-Bee's colors and laughing with Mrs. McKenna. But none of that changed the fact that her father was in love with Miss Hogan and that no matter how much she wanted to, Melody would never, ever know the person who had felt her kicking inside her like a little kangaroo.

Chapter Twenty

When she came in the house, the first thing Melody noticed were her father's muddy boots lying on the floor.

"Dad?" she called.

"In here, Mel!"

"What are you doing home?" she asked, joining him in the kitchen, where he was making himself a sandwich.

"In a nutshell — the camping trip got rained out, my car broke down on the way home and had to be towed to the shop, and I will never go anywhere that involves teenagers, tents, and canned beans again. And how was *your* weekend?"

He meant to be funny, but Melody wasn't amused. There was something she needed to get off her chest.

"In a nutshell," she said, "Nick and Gramp-o got food poisoning, and I discovered that just because your father knows the definition of a word, it doesn't mean he knows how to apply it to his own life."

Melody's father looked confused.

"You lost me," he said.

"*Unilaterally* means doing something without taking into account how another person might feel about it, right?"

"Have I done something to hurt your feelings, Mel?"

"That depends. Does sneaking around behind my back dating my teacher count?" she asked.

Melody watched the color drain from her father's face. Any hope that she might have had that she was mistaken about Miss Hogan and her father drained away, too. She couldn't believe it. This was really happening. Miss Hogan was actually going to marry her father.

"How did you find out?" he asked.

"I heard you talking to her on the phone. You called her *honey*, and then you lied and told me it was a wrong number. *Remember?*"

Melody's father hung his head, exactly the way Teeny Nelson had done when her mother had yelled at her for going into the Bishops' yard without being invited first.

"I didn't want to tell you about the relationship until I was sure it was serious," Melody's father told her. "I certainly didn't mean for you to find out like this. I'm so sorry, Mel."

Melody wasn't ready to accept his apology.

"How could you do this to me?" she asked. "Don't you care about how I feel?"

"Of course I do," said her father. "To be honest, I expected you to be happy about this news."

Just when Melody thought she couldn't feel any worse, her father had to go and say that. Was he so head-over-heels in love with Miss Hogan he'd forgotten how Melody felt about her?

"*Happy?*" she said, and she was practically yelling now. "Why would I be happy? This is the worst thing that's ever happened to me. You're ruining my life and you don't even care."

"Now wait a minute." Melody's father reached over and tried to touch her hand.

Melody jerked it away.

"No, *you* wait a minute!" she shouted. "How could you think this would be okay with me? You didn't even ask. You just went ahead and did what you wanted to do, without even thinking about how I'd feel. Why do you get to decide everything? How much TV I watch. What kind of cereal I can eat. You even get to decide how much I know about my own mother. And now, without even consulting me, you get to decide *this*? It's not fair!"

Melody couldn't hold back her tears any longer.

"Please don't cry, Mel," said her father.

"Why shouldn't I cry?" she said through her tears. "You're going to marry Miss Hogan."

Melody's father's jaw dropped.

"Miss Hogan?" he said incredulously. "Is that who you think I've been seeing?"

"Well, isn't it?" asked Melody.

Her father smacked his forehead with the heel of his hand.

"No wonder you're so upset. I wouldn't do that to you, Mel," he said. "Good grief! I wouldn't do that to *me*."

"Then why did Miss Hogan know you'd gone camping?" asked Melody.

"Her nephew Kirk is on the debate team."

"Why was she whistling your song?"

"What song?" Melody's father asked.

But Melody had already moved on to her next question — the most important one of all.

"If you're not going out with Miss Hogan, then who have you been seeing?"

"MaryAnn McKenna."

It took a minute for it to register.

"Mrs. McKenna?" asked Melody. "But she's married."

"She was, but her husband passed away a few years ago. She kept his name out of respect."

Melody had to ask again, just to make sure she hadn't misunderstood.

"So the person you called *honey* on the phone the other night wasn't Miss Hogan, it was Mrs. McKenna?"

Melody's father smiled. "That's right."

"I *love* Mrs. McKenna!" cried Melody, grabbing her father and hugging him tight.

"I know," he said, hugging her back. "So do I."

That night the Bishops ordered a pizza for dinner. Gramp-o, who was feeling much better, came downstairs to join them, but he stuck to ginger ale and saltines just to be safe. He was almost as happy to hear about Mrs. McKenna as Melody had been.

"An excellent choice, son," he said. "On both of your parts."

The pizza arrived and Melody's father paid the delivery boy. As he carried the pizza into the dining room, he started whistling again.

"I guess it was just a coincidence that Miss Hogan was whistling that song yesterday," said Melody. "But is there something special about 'You Are My Sunshine' to you, Dad?"

Melody saw tears start to well up in his eyes.

"It was one of your mother's favorites," he said. "She always sang it when she was happy. I hope wherever she is, she's singing it now."

"Me too," said Melody.

After dinner, Melody and her father wrapped up the leftover pizza in tinfoil and put it in the freezer. Then they sat down together and had a long talk. She told him all about the quest she and Nick had gone on to find out who *honey* might be, about her two visits to the Bee Hive, and about listening to the recording of her mother playing the piano, too.

"That's the tape you played at Mom's funeral, isn't it?" she asked.

"How did you know about that?" her father replied.

"Bee-Bee told me. She was there and she said I was there, too."

"I'm sorry if it made you sad to listen to the tape."

"I'm not sorry," said Melody. "I wish I could have met Mom, but at least now I know what her voice sounded like."

"I only wanted to protect you," said her father.

"I know. But I want to know who she was. I need to know."

"There are some videos up in the attic," her father told her. "I'll bring them down and we can watch them together tomorrow if you want. It's Memorial Day, so there's no school on Monday. There's also a box of stuff I saved from when you were a baby, including a beautiful little pink blanket your mother crocheted for you. I wrapped you up in that blanket the day you were born and put you in your mother's arms so she could say good-bye to you."

Melody lay her head on her father's chest. She could hear his heart beating. She closed her eyes. This time, instead of red, she saw mossy greens and deep-sea blues. Her father put his arms around her and they were sad together for a while.

"Promise me something," Melody said later, when her father came in to say good night. "No more secrets."

"I promise," he told her.

That night, as Melody lay sleeping in her bed, her father climbed the narrow steps to the attic and brought down all the things he'd promised to show Melody. Then he added one more thing to the pile, a small blue box, which he'd been keeping hidden in the back of a dresser drawer. He had told Melody there would be no more secrets, and he intended to keep his promise.

Chapter Twenty-One

The next morning, Melody called Nick to give him the good news.

"*Mrs. McKenna?*" he cried. "You lucky duck!"

"I know," said Melody, "I still can't believe it. I've been pinching myself so much my arms are covered with bruises."

"Wait," said Nick. "So if your dad is in love with Mrs. McKenna, then who is Miss Hogan marrying?"

"Who cares?" said Melody. "As long as it isn't my father."

"Tell your dad congratulations, and tell him I'm sorry I ralphed on his couch, too. And, Bishop?"

"Yeah, Woo?"

"I'm glad you don't have to move to Siberia."

"Me too," said Melody.

There was one other person Melody wanted to tell. She went to look for her father and found him in his office, grading papers.

"Hey, Dad," she said, sticking her head in the door. "Nick and I pulled out twenty-five dandelions on Saturday. Can you think of anywhere I could buy a nice candy dish for a dollar and twenty-five cents?"

"Don't you mean a dollar and point two-five cents?" he teased. "Why do you need a candy dish?"

"It's for Bee-Bee," she said. "Hers got broken yesterday. I'm going to ride over to the Bee Hive this morning, and I thought maybe I could bring it to her."

Melody got the sense that her father wasn't exactly thrilled with her plan.

"I was hoping you and I could spend a little time together this morning, Mel," he said. "I brought down that box of stuff from the attic."

"Can it wait until later, Dad?" she asked. "I really want to tell Bee-Bee about Mrs. McKenna."

"I suppose," he said. "But don't stay too long, okay? We need to make a grocery list. MaryAnn has offered to come over tonight and make dinner for us."

"Really?" said Melody. She had to pinch herself again.

"She asked me to find out what you'd like her to make."

"Tell her anything would be fine," said Melody. "As long as it isn't tuna noodle casserole."

Gramp-o's car was still sitting in the driveway. Melody's father would have to rely on Esmeralda for a few days until his car was out of the shop. As she went into the garage to get her bike, Melody noticed an old fishbowl sitting in the corner of the garage and realized it would make a perfect replacement for Bee-Bee's candy bowl. As she started down the driveway with the fishbowl balanced carefully on her handlebars, she heard a familiar voice.

"*Knock-knock!*" Teeny Nelson called through the knothole in the fence.

Melody was in such a good mood, she didn't even hesitate before calling back.

"Who's there?"

Teeny scrambled up to the top of the fence.

"Orange juice," she said with a wide grin.

"Orange juice who?" asked Melody.

"Orange juice glad to see me?"

"Actually, I am," she told Teeny.

"You are?" asked Teeny, surprised.

"I've been wondering how things went with your mother when she found out you'd torn your tutu."

Teeny stuck a grubby finger in her mouth and wiggled a loose tooth.

"At first Mama got mad," she said. "Then when I told her about going to the Bee Hive by myself she got even madder."

"Did you get a spanking?" asked Melody, sincerely hoping she hadn't.

"Nope," Teeny told her. "Mama said she was proud of me for telling the truth and she said if I'm a good girl, next time she gets her fingernails painted, I can get mine done, too."

"In case you're still planning to get number fifty-four, you should know it's got a new name," said Melody.

"What is it?" asked Teeny.

"You'll see."

"You want to hear another knock-knock joke?" Teeny asked. "I've got a whole bunch."

"Maybe later."

"What are you going to do with that fishbowl?" asked Teeny.

"I'm taking it to a friend."

"What kind of fish does your friend have?"

"Swedish Fish," said Melody.

Teeny didn't get the joke. Sensing Melody was

about to leave, she blurted out, "I know something you don't know! It's about Henry and the love bug."

"I don't care about that anymore," Melody told Teeny.

"I do. Mama says if I'm a *really* good girl, maybe we can get one of the kittens."

Melody's interest was piqued. "What kittens?" she asked.

Teeny started wiggling her tooth again.

"I thought you said you didn't care about it anymore," she said.

"Tell me about the kittens, and I'll bring you something special when I come back," Melody offered.

"What are you going to bring me?"

"Tell me first."

It turned out that there was another Henry in Royal, after all: a large orange cat — the same one that had been hanging around the Bee Hive lately. It was *this* Henry who had been bitten by the love bug. He belonged to the pharmacist's sister, Mrs. James, who was a friend of Mrs. Nelson's. Apparently Teeny had overheard the two of them talking about how Henry had taken a shine to the neighbor's calico, Josephine, and the result had been a litter of ten adorable kittens.

"Don't forget to bring me something!" Teeny hollered after Melody as she rode off.

· · ·

When Melody arrived at the Bee Hive, she found a sign hanging in the window saying it was closed. She was just about to turn around and ride home when Bee-Bee flung open the door.

"Melody!" she called out to her. "What a nice surprise. Come on in."

Bee-Bee's hair was red again, only this time it was straight and hung down to her waist, swaying like a grass hula skirt when she moved. She was wearing an apron and rubber gloves, and there were wet towels and soap suds all over the floor of the salon.

"What happened?" asked Melody. "Did your washing machine explode or something?"

"My dog got so muddy yesterday I decided to give him a bath in the shampoo sink," Bee-Bee explained. "As you can see, he put up quite a fight."

"Where is he now?" asked Melody, looking around.

"He's in the apartment, hiding under the bed."

Melody handed Bee-Bee the fishbowl and explained what it was for.

"It's perfect!" Bee-Bee exclaimed. "Even better than the first one."

She got a sponge and washed the fishbowl out with soap and hot water. When she was finished she put it on the counter and filled it to the top with candy.

"Do you mind if I take a couple of Dum Dums for Teeny?" Melody asked. "I promised I would bring her something."

"Take as many as you want," Bee-Bee told her. "But first tell me what you think."

Bee-Bee held out her hands. Her fingernails were painted to look like bees.

"Cool!" said Melody.

"I've been practicing all morning trying to get the stripes right. I've never really done nail art before, but now I'm totally hooked."

Melody dug around in the fishbowl until she found a root beer and a mystery flavor Dum Dum and tucked them into the pocket of her jeans. She spotted a cherry Starburst — her favorite flavor — and snagged it for herself for later.

"I have some good news," she told Bee-Bee. "My dad isn't marrying Miss Hogan after all."

She told Bee-Bee about Mrs. McKenna.

"This calls for a celebration!" Bee-Bee said, and she grabbed Melody by the hand and pulled her over to the closet where she kept her wigs.

"Pick one," she told Melody. "Something to match your mood."

Melody hesitated.

"I don't know if I really want to," she said.

"Come on," Bee-Bee told her, "it'll be fun." She grabbed a blond wig off of one of the Styrofoam heads and helped Melody put it on. "Go look at yourself in the mirror while I put on some music."

Melody walked over to the mirror and stared at the girl with the long yellow hair. Maybe she wasn't the spitting image of her mother, but for the first time, Melody could see the resemblance, and she was really glad about it.

Bee-Bee put on some early Beatles and started dancing, pushing towels around with her feet to dry the wet floor.

"Come dance with me, Melody," she called. "And afterward we'll make you a special polish with all the happy colors in it."

Melody already knew what she was going to name her color — Honey.

But the polish would have to wait for another day. As the Beatles launched into a chorus of "I Want to Hold Your Hand," the door opened and Melody's father stepped into the salon. When he saw Melody in the wig, he did a double take.

"What's going on in here?" he shouted over the music.

"We're celebrating," Melody shouted back.

Bee-Bee went and turned off the music.

"Hello, Henry," she said, kissing Melody's father on the cheek. "It's good to see you."

"I'm sorry," he said. "I probably should have called first. I didn't mean to interrupt the fun. Are those bees on your fingernails?"

He seemed nervous. Melody noticed his hands were shaking a little.

"What are you doing here, Dad?" she asked. "Is everything okay? Gramp-o's not sick again, is he?"

"Is there someplace we can talk?" he said. "The three of us?"

Now Bee-Bee seemed nervous, too.

"The salon doesn't open today until noon," she said. "No one will bother us. Come on in and have a seat, Henry."

"What's going on?" Melody asked as she sat down beside her father on the wicker bench. Bee-Bee pulled up a chair and sat opposite them.

Melody's father took a deep breath. Then he reached into his pocket and took out a small blue box.

"There's something I need to tell you, Mel," he said.

Chapter Twenty-Two

"I'm going to tell you a story," Melody's father said. "And I want you to let me finish before you ask any questions. Okay?"

"Okay," said Melody.

"Are you sure you want to do this, Henry?" Bee-Bee asked. "You don't have to, you know."

"Yes, I do," said Melody's father.

He began by telling Melody that one day, about a month or so before she was born, her mother had told him she wanted to go for a drive out in the country, to get some fresh air.

"I remember she was wearing a yellow dress that day," Melody's father said. "Because her belly was so big by then, instead of trying to squeeze into our little VW bug, we decided to ask your grandfather if we could borrow his car."

The car was brand-new, right off the lot. Melody's mother and father had climbed into the shiny white sedan and headed off for what was supposed to have been an impromptu drive in the country.

"I should have known your mother was up to something," said Melody's father.

Melody's mother had read an article in the paper about a puppy mill out near Cloverhitch that had fallen on hard times.

"Your mother loved animals, Mel, especially dogs. And she had this idea that a family wasn't complete without one. I'd never owned a pet, and did my best to talk her out of it, but she was a force to be reckoned with — just like you."

The paper had run a picture along with the article, and in it there was a tiny brown-and-white puppy with pointy ears and bowed legs.

"Your mother got her heart set on having that dog and I couldn't bear to disappoint her. A few hours later, when we got back to Royal, he was sitting in the backseat, panting and wagging his curled-up little tail. He was the runt of the litter, all skin and bones, but your mother fattened him up in no time at all. She spoiled him rotten, too."

Melody had managed to listen quietly up to this point in the story, but she had to ask.

"Did something happen to the puppy?"

"Hang on," said her father. "We'll get there, I promise."

He explained that Melody's mother had been crazy about the dog. Her eyes lit up every time she saw him, and clearly the feeling was mutual. He followed her everywhere she went.

Melody's father paused. The next part of the story would be hard for him to tell.

"The day you were born I was so busy trying to take care of you, and your mother, I forgot all about the dog. I didn't feed him, or walk him, and when he came upstairs looking for your mother, I scolded him and told him to go away."

"You were overwhelmed," said Bee-Bee.

"Yes," said Melody's father. "You were so tiny, Mel, and your poor mother . . ." He shook his head. "I couldn't handle it. So a few days later, when a kind friend stepped in and offered to take care of the dog, just for a little while, I thought it would be best for everyone if I let him go."

"Just for a little while, though, right?" asked Melody.

"That was the original plan. But then that little while turned into a long while and —"

"You left him there, Dad?"

"He was in good hands. Better hands than mine would have been."

"But he must have been wondering where you were and what had happened to Mom," said Melody.

Her father looked at Bee-Bee again.

"I wouldn't have said anything, Henry," Bee-Bee told him. "I gave you my word."

"I know, Bee-Bee, and I truly appreciate everything you've done, but I promised Melody I wouldn't keep any more secrets from her."

"What are you talking about?" asked Melody. "What secret?"

"A few weeks ago, this same kind friend called me up on the phone and told me she was moving here to Royal," Melody's father said.

"Did she bring the dog with her?" asked Melody anxiously.

Her father nodded. "He's here."

Melody's anxiety instantly turned to excitement. "Can we go see him? What's his name?"

"If it had been up to me, I would have picked something literary, like Tolstoy or Hemingway, but he was your mother's dog and she wanted to name him after one of her favorite composers."

"Brahms?" guessed Melody, remembering the name written on the tape.

"No," said her father. "Wolfgang Amadeus Mozart."

Melody laughed. "That's an awfully long name for a little puppy."

"That's why we gave him a nickname," said her father, handing Melody the blue box.

Inside, between two squares of soft cotton, was a tarnished silver chain. Melody lifted it out of the box and read the name inscribed on the little heart-shaped pendant.

"Mo."

Chapter Twenty-Three

Mo was not happy. Why had the tall woman felt the need to give him a bath that morning? What was so special about today that required that he be any cleaner than he'd been the day before? He hoped she would make it up to him later by cooking him something nice for supper. It was the least she could do after what he'd been through.

Once he was sure the coast was clear, he crawled out from under the bed and went into the kitchen for a drink of water. When he was done, he lifted his nose and sniffed. The scent of new-cut grass was stronger than ever. Cocking his head to one side, he listened intently. Someone was coming.

The door opened . . . and as soon as he saw the

girl standing there, it all came rushing back to him. The large woman with her hair spread out on the pillow like a halo behind her, the thin man with glasses, and the small gray bundle on the bed.

At least, it had looked gray to Mo. *Of course*, he thought. That's who this girl was — the bundle, now standing before him, no longer small, but still smelling sweetly of new-cut grass. The light caught in her long yellow hair, and when she threw back her head and laughed, Mo's breath quickened and his heart began to race. She opened her hand and there was the heart-shaped pendant, dangling from her fingers on the silver chain.

Mo heard the jingle-jangle and knew where he was meant to be.

The girl looked at him with wide eyes. "It's you," she whispered. Then she ran to him and threw her arms around his neck.

The phone call Bee-Bee Churchill had made that day at the Frosty Boy while the real estate agent waited outside had been to Melody's father. She'd wanted to ask if it would be a problem for him if she and Mo came to live in Royal. It had been a long time since they'd spoken, and Henry Bishop admitted that he'd never told Melody about the dog because he thought it might upset her. Bee-Bee had promised to keep his secret.

The only reason she had let Teeny Nelson visit Mo was because she knew Teeny wouldn't have any way to make a connection between Melody and Mo. Later, when Teeny and Melody showed up at the Bee Hive together, and Teeny asked to see the dog again, Bee-Bee didn't want to take any chances. She had promised Henry his secret was safe with her.

Melody and her father were both grateful to Bee-Bee for taking such good care of Mo.

"It was my pleasure," she told them. "But now it's time for him to go home."

"But he's your dog," said Melody.

"Just for a little while," said Bee-Bee. "That was the deal. Even Mo knows that. It's clear from the way he's looking at you, he's been waiting for you to come and find him all along."

"Won't you miss him?" Melody asked.

"Sure I will. But he can come and visit anytime — I'll be right here. And, to tell you the truth, I've always been more of a cat person."

Melody had an idea. "Mrs. James, the pharmacist's sister, has a cat who just had a litter of kittens. Maybe you could have one of them."

"I might just take a walk over there later today and have a look," said Bee-Bee.

Melody's father was staring at her.

"It's uncanny how much you look like your mother in that thing," he said, pointing to her hair.

In all the excitement, Melody had completely forgotten about the wig. While she went and put it back in the closet, Bee-Bee gathered up Mo's things, and Melody's father loaded her bike into Esmeralda's trunk, tying it closed with a rope.

"You're a good boy, Mo," Bee-Bee said, scratching him under the chin. "Come by whenever you like. I promise to make you chicken and dumplings and never to give you a bath again."

The next thing he knew, Mo was sitting in the backseat of the old white car. The thin man with glasses kept glancing in the rearview mirror at him and the little girl sang, *You are my sunshine, my only sunshine . . .* in a high clear voice as they headed down the road together toward home.

Melody's Nail Polish Names:

#1: *Silver Linings*

#2: *Cherry Pie*

#3: *Emerald City*

#4: *Pink Frosting*

#5: *Queen Anne's Lace*

#6: *Red Badge of Courage*

#7: *Holy Moly!*

#8: *Gingersnap*

#9: *Shooting Star*

#10: *Ectoplasmic Ooze*

#11: *Maple Syrup*

#12: *Daffodil*

#13: *Hot Cocoa*

#14: *Kitten Nose*

#15: *Fancy Fingers*

#16: *Cinnamon Sugar*

#17: *Wintergreen*

#18: *Whitecap*

#19: *Moonlight*

#20: *Royal Plum*

#21: *Your Majesty*

#22: *Glamourpuss*

#23: *Blue Jay*

#24: *Sunset*

#25: *A Whisper of Smoke*

#26: *Wild Berry Skittles*

#27: *Watermelon*

#28: *Ladybug*

#29: *Tutti-Frutti*

#30: *Sea Glass*

#31: *Let's Go, Kokomo!*

#32: *Toasted Marshmallow*

#33: *Rosy Cheeks*

#34: *Starburst*

#35: *Snow Angel*

#36: *Pacific Ocean*

#37: *Ripe Papaya*

#38: *Pillow Fight*

#39: *Root Beer Dum Dum*

#40: *Cotton Candy*

#41: *Slumber Party*

#42: *Dandy-Lion*

#43: *Confetti*

#44: *Swimming Pool*

#45: *Whipped Cream*

#46: *Sweet Dreams*

#47: *Pearly Gates*

#48: *Icicle*

#49: *Pink Lemonade*

#50: *Love Bug*

#51: *Grape Jelly*

#52: *Queen of Hearts*

#53: *Eureka!*

#54: *Teeny's Tutu*

#55: *Surf's Up!*

#56: *April Showers*

#57: *May Flowers*

#58: *Red Licorice*

#59: *Orange Marmalade*

#60: *Seashell*

#61: *Lemon Drop*

#62: *Raspberry Jam*

#63: *White Tulips*

#64: *Banana Split*

#65: *Pink Flamingo*

#66: *Diamond Ring*

#67: *String of Pearls*

#68: *Cool as a Cucumber*

#69: *Tidal Wave*

#70: *Red Hots*

#71: *Be Mine, Valentine*

#72: *Fireworks*

#73: *All That Glitters*

#74: *Candy Apple*

#75: *Wild Strawberries*

#76: *Little Red Wagon*

#77: *Christmas Tinsel*

#78: *Candy Kiss*

#79: *Pot of Gold*

#80: *Snow Globe*

#81: *Lucky Penny*

#82: *Zippity Doo Dah*

#83: *Sweet Potato*

#84: *Fire Engine*

#85: *Roses Are Red*

#86: *Silver Bullet*

#87: *Milk Dud*

#88: *Midas Touch*

#89: *Kaboom!*

#90: *Velveeta*

#91: *Tomato Soup*

#92: *Brahms Intermezzo*

#93: *Fuzzy Pink Slippers*

#94: *Fireball*

#95: *Creamsicle*

#96: *Esmeralda*

#97: *Orange You Glad to See Me?*

#98: *Silver Heart*

#99: *Annabelle's Bubble*

#100: *You Are My Sunshine*

#101: *Honey*

Acknowledgments

There are many people who helped me with this story — Jim Fyfe, Frances Weeks, Nathaniel Abbott, Gabriel Abbott, Lucia Gratch, Abby Gaebel, Parrish Finn, Barrett Rollins — but there would be no *HONEY* were it not for my brilliant and patient editor, David Levithan. Thank you, David, for knowing when to leave me be and when to take me by the hand and lead me out of the darkness.

— SW

Sarah Weeks did extensive research for the making of this book, including making her own nail polish from scratch. She's delighted to report that when she does school visits, the boys seem as eager to try polishing their nails as the girls.

When not brainstorming names for new nail polish colors or painting her toenails to look like bumblebees, Sarah writes widely acclaimed novels, including *Save Me a Seat* (with Gita Varadarajan); *Pie*; *So B. It*; *Cheese: A Combo of "Oggie Cooder" and "Oggie Cooder, Party Animal"*; and *As Simple as It Seems*. She lives in New York and can be found on the Web at www.sarahweeks.com.

Stories of family, friendship, and finding yourself... from award-winning author Sarah Weeks!